# WOLF'S TEMPTATION

## GUARDED BY THE SHIFTER
### BOOK FIVE

## KATE RUDOLPH

# ABOUT WOLF'S TEMPTATION

When a rescue mission goes wrong and Erin Jackson is abducted by a mysterious enemy, Jericho Gibson will stop at nothing to bring her home. But reuniting her with the rest of their pack is easier said than done when dark magic hunts them on their journey up the eastern seaboard.

Erin and Gibson have spent years denying the pull between them, but with emotions running high, and no one there to run interference, there's no avoiding the inferno of passion that threatens to consume them.

But passion is not their problem. A dark force is stalking them, and if they don't find its source, no one will be safe.

# PROLOGUE

*Six Months Ago*

Gibson traced the condensation on the beer bottle clutched between his hands and wondered what the hell he was doing at some hipster bar in Brooklyn. He'd never heard of the brand he was drinking and was a bit disgusted at how delicious it was. Pretentious things weren't actually supposed to be *good*.

But it was Owen's birthday, and he had to make an appearance. Hell, even the rock star had shown up, though she was hiding in a corner wearing an obnoxious baseball cap that wasn't doing much to hide the fact that millions of people bought her records.

He was the old fart sitting at the bar and

bringing down the mood. He swirled the liquid in the bottle and figured he could sneak out in ten minutes and call it good. Owen was celebrating with his arm around his mate, and Gibson didn't think he'd ever seen Stasia smile that broadly. The doctor was good for Owen, and maybe he was good for her.

"The party's over there," Erin Jackson said as she slid onto the barstool next to him.

Even in the crowded bar he caught a hint of her scent, something floral with a tinge of the ocean underneath it. He tilted his beer at her in greeting but didn't let himself fully turn to look at her. He knew what he'd see: blonde hair held back in a tight braid, wide blue eyes that hid a hint of mischief that no one seemed to notice, curves that made his blood heat no matter how much he tried to ignore them. Tonight she wore a short dress that kissed the top of her thighs.

If he looked at her, he wouldn't be able to hide the hunger.

So Gibson kept looking at the bar. "No one needs the boss ruining a good time." He offered her half a grin and a shrug, as if the wall he kept between himself and his people never bothered him. Gibson didn't regret taking responsibility for his strange little pack of wolves, but sometimes the chasm between them was just as impossible to breach as that between officer and enlisted.

"You're more than our boss." She said it quietly, and it was enough to make Gibson look over, but Jackson had flagged down the bartender and wasn't looking at him.

He was fooling himself if he thought he heard something more when she spoke. He was on the wrong side of forty, she was more than ten years younger than him, he'd been an officer while she was enlisted, and he was her god damned boss.

This impulse he felt, the need to reach out and feel her soft skin against his, was impossible. Jackson didn't want him, didn't need him.

"Shouldn't you be over there with the rest of them?" Owen let out a shrieking hoot that had half the bar glancing his way.

Jackson gave him a look that said more than words ever could. "He threatened to order shots. Not exactly my scene."

"No?" He didn't ask her what she did like. That way led to danger.

"Not really." She sipped her own glass of beer. "I know Owen's happy you came. He wanted the whole... you know, all of us, to be here." She tripped over the word *pack*.

Gibson understood. If anyone tried calling him an alpha, he wasn't sure what he'd do. They were just a bunch of unfortunate soldiers; none of them had signed up for this werewolf shit. "I should get going."

"Or you could play me in that giant Jenga game over there." She nodded towards a quieter corner of the bar, far away from Owen and his threatened shots.

He knew he shouldn't. Every moment spent with Erin Jackson left him craving more. It was something he could ignore on the job. There, they had a purpose. But here? Cut off from the rest of the group and playing a game made it feel a bit like a date.

Still, he found himself sliding off the barstool and following her to where the tower was already set up.

"Did you plan this?" he asked. "Are you some sort of Jenga genius?"

Jackson laughed, and the sound went right to his gut. "You caught me, I'm a Jenga prodigy. Now, are we going to make this interesting?"

"Hell no. I'm keeping my money safe from you." The banter came easy, even if his instincts were screaming at him to walk away.

"That's not the only way to make it interesting."

She grinned, then her eyes widened and she clamped her mouth shut.

But she said it.

And he heard it.

And he knew.

Erin Jackson wasn't flirty. She was the most professional member of his team, except maybe for Andre. She always said what she meant and she didn't play around.

Gibson wanted to say something back, wanted to crowd her up against the wall and see how she reacted when their bodies pressed tightly together, the need clear in every breath of his being.

Instead, he forced himself to ignore the taunt. "Let's play."

Her comment wasn't forgotten. It lay over them with every move, but as the blocks dwindled and their tower became more and more precarious, Gibson let himself get lost in the game. When he played, he played to win.

But not this time.

The tower was perched on one block, and it wobbled every time someone stepped too close to the table. He didn't have any good options to remove, and Jackson was staring at him with a triumphant gleam in her eye, clearly convinced the she was about to win.

Gibson circled the table, trying to find the one block he could remove without crashing the whole thing down around them. He ended up right next to Jackson, who didn't budge from where she was standing, probably to make it harder for him to remove his block. He poked at it, carefully displacing it, not daring to breathe as it moved millimeter by millimeter out of position.

He thought he had it. The thing was almost completely out, and all he had to do was move it the final little bit.

But something went wrong, and between one breath and the next, the entire tower was crashing towards them. On instinct, Gibson flung his arms around Jackson and pushed her back.

Her own arms went around his, her body flush against him, soft in all the right places and so damned tempting that he almost threw all caution to the wind and captured her lips with his own. He could do it. He could probably even call it an accident if it blew up in his face.

He could feel her fingers curl into his jacket, the edges of her knuckles resting against his back.

What would it feel like if her nails were scraping down his back?

Gibson looked down. Jackson looked up. Their eyes locked, and the rest of the room fell away. All he could see, all he could hear, all he could smell was her. Her scent wrapped around him, alluring as hell and so damned perfect that he had to bite back a groan.

Jackson's tongue darted out to wet her lips and her mouth opened, so close and inviting he could practically taste it.

All one of them had to do was lean forward. One kiss and it would end this suffering, this clawing *need* he couldn't slake.

One kiss and they'd ruin everything.

Gibson stepped back, nearly tripping over a fallen block but righting himself before he fell flat on his ass. "Good game," he said. "Tell Owen I had to take off."

And he left without looking back.

# CHAPTER ONE

The smell of fish was overwhelming. It made Erin Jackson's stomach turn, and she had to swallow down her puke. Her clothes were already encrusted in blood. She didn't want to make things worse.

Her stomach roiled again.

No. Not her stomach. Her everything.

She cracked her eyes open, and for a second, thought she'd been blinded.

But, no, it was just dark. Her eyes adjusted quickly.

Metal. Low ceiling. Long, narrow room. And that incessant movement. Up and down. High, then low, enough to make her head spin.

She was on a ship. Possibly out at sea.

If that was true, it meant no one was coming for her.

Erin slumped even further in her seat, only her handcuffs and bound feet keeping her from sliding off.

She needed to find her own way out of this place, or she was a dead woman.

Pulling against the handcuffs was harder than it should have been. She had a decade or more of serious weight training under her belt, not to mention a bit of extra that came from her shifter strength.

But all of her muscles were heavy and exhausted. How long had she been chained to this chair?

The ship roiled again, and Erin gagged.

The last thing she remembered was the mission to retrieve Owen. In the chaos of the escape, she hadn't seen her attacker coming. One blow to the back of her head, and she was out.

Erin rolled her head from one side to the other and was relieved not to feel a throb of pain. Maybe she didn't have a concussion.

Could shifters even get concussions?

Given how her thoughts were swirling around, none quite willing to settle into something actionable, Erin feared it might be so. She stilled herself, letting her bound hands fall behind her back in as comfortable a position as possible.

Assessment.

Dried blood. She'd been taken some time ago. She ached, but nothing had the acute feel of an open wound. And she couldn't even be sure it was her blood.

She ran her tongue over her lips. Dry and cracked, but not cut.

Light. It flickered in through a cracked window high on the wall. She'd been knocked out at night, so that meant it had been at least seven hours, provided she was still in New York.

She strained to hear anything, but all she could make out was water and crying birds. She wasn't sure what a port sounded like, but weren't there supposed to be braying horns and the general clang of commerce?

Erin put it out of her mind. Wherever she was, she'd deal with that after she got free and took her frustration out on whoever thought they got to just hold her captive.

She gave the cuffs on her hands a good yank, but all that did was bite into the sensitive, bruised skin around her wrists. That didn't stop her from trying to tug her hand through the metal circle.

It was useless. She'd need to shear off a thumb to make it work.

That sparked an idea almost too ludicrous to consider.

Could she...?

Erin nearly dismissed the thought out of hand. She knew her limits.

But limits were the kind of thing that kept a girl chained to a chair. And Erin had never let a thing as stupid as someone else's limit stop her before.

As far as she and the rest of her pack knew, a shifter had two states: human and wolf. But they'd been learning by trial and error for the past three years. And the line between what they "knew" and what was possible blurred more and more every day.

Erin had to get out of the cuffs. She didn't have a key or anything else to jimmy the lock. And she didn't plan to wait around for someone to come find her.

There was a wildness deep inside of her that Erin tried to ignore. She had a job to do, and changing into wolf wasn't going to help anything. But now she needed that wildness, needed the streak of anger and fangs that lurked in the darkness at the edge of her consciousness, ready to strike whenever she let her guard down.

Erin closed her eyes and took a deep breath. The stench of blood and saltwater threatened to over-whelm her, but she pushed it aside and breathed again. There was nothing in the moment except her and the swaying of the boat.

She wiggled her fingers, trying not to wince as blood rushed into the neglected limbs. The pain made her feel every inch of the skin, for better or worse. And that was what she needed.

But not fingers.

Claws.

She clenched her fingers together and imagined her other form. It was a strange thing to do. She didn't look in a mirror when she wore her fur; she didn't care what she looked like.

Normally, switching between forms was as easy as breathing. But with her arms yanked back, she didn't know what that would do to her wolfish joints. She just needed one paw.

Erin ran her thumb over the pad of her fingers, and only felt a human hand.

Frustration surged through her, but she wasn't giving up that easily.

And so what if she turned all the way? She'd be out of the chair.

And possibly broken beyond repair.

Damn it! She needed to stop thinking about problems. Now was the time for solutions.

*Give me a damn paw.*

A jolt of awareness flashed up her arm, similar to the pins and needles flinch of when a limb fell asleep. Her hand cramped and the pain seared through her blood. Erin choked back a yelp as she felt the metal of the handcuff slip.

Then stick.

What the hell?

She brushed her hands together and felt fur and skin, the feeling disorienting. It took all her concentration to hold her paw in that form, and the handcuff still wasn't falling off.

How big were her damned paws?

She yanked her shoulder forward and gasped as the cuff scraped over her fur and off her wrist. Her hands were free, and tension and lactic acid flooded her shoulders in another wave of pain.

Her concentration shattered, and by the time she looked down at her hands, they both looked human, though the nails on her left hand were a bit longer than usual.

A loud thump reverberated through the metal walls of the room and Erin froze, waiting for the threat to show itself. A second thump on the other side of the ship split her attention, and she quivered with anticipation.

Nothing came.

She was caught between holding still and scrambling to free her legs. Freeing her legs won. They were tied together with a massive length of rope, but luckily they weren't secured to the chair. It took several frustrating minutes to work her way to the end of a piece of rope and start to unravel the knot.

But her fingernails were still sharper than usual.

Erin dug into the rope, wincing as it tore at her skin and nails, but it didn't take long before she hit a vital piece of the knot and the whole thing gave.

She kicked the rope aside and stood, staggering as the ship roiled again. The chair fell to the wayside, and Erin had to brace with wide feet to keep from falling. Whoever said sea legs were a thing was a dirty liar.

Well. She was out of the chair. What next?

The room was disorientingly big, like she was in the middle of a steel walled warehouse that was completely empty. She expected someone in a catwalk on the ceiling to stop her, but no one was there.

She hadn't seen a single person.

Was it possible she was alone?

No. Definitely not. Erin wasn't the lucky type, and she couldn't believe she'd be taken only to be abandoned at sea like some misbehaving pirate in an old movie.

She had to get out of this room and find a way off the boat and back to her pack. Had the pack found Owen? Was he okay?

It was easier to care about someone else's problems.

The walls were solid steel, but rusty. She was tempted to give them a good kick, but even the rust looked stronger than it should have. If it could withstand the battering of the ocean, it would handle her, no problem.

She searched for her escape and... there! The freaking door.

There was a weird lever that she had to pull from one side to the other instead of a handle or a latch, but she figured it out quickly, and she had to bite back a shout of joy when the door opened.

Unlocked.

Maybe her luck was turning around.

Cold sea air rushed in, along with daylight strong enough to blind her. Erin didn't care. She wasn't tied up. She wasn't locked up. Who needed eyesight?

Even the air tasted delicious. Anything would, when it washed away the smell of blood.

But the light and air weren't hitting her directly. The door opened into a small, windy hallway. Erin turned right, because she had to choose a direction and hesitating wouldn't get her home any sooner.

The sounds of water slapping against metal grew louder, and the wall beside her ended to reveal water going on for miles. And, in the distance, a city.

Erin squinted. And then she cursed.

She might have been quite a ways from the coast, but who couldn't recognize the New York City skyline?

Whatever city lay out there, it wasn't New York.

Shit.

That was a problem for future Erin. She didn't care if that city was in freaking Narnia, she'd have a better shot of getting home if she was on land rather than the sea.

She peered over the edge of the ship and was struck by sudden vertigo, her stomach churning once more.

It was a long drop. Long.

And she might have some sort of werewolf superpowers, but there was a limit to what she'd try. If she jumped, she wouldn't survive the fall. And, on the off chance she did survive, she'd be in no condition to swim miles to shore.

She needed to call for help. Or find a way off the ship that didn't involve a hundred foot drop into the arms of Scylla and Charybdis.

Erin kept moving. She still hadn't seen anyone, but someone had to be piloting the ship. She'd bet all she was worth—not that she was worth much—that the pilot was in on it. A girl didn't end up tied up in a cargo hold by accident.

She almost walked right into a cluster of crew, but voices echoed her way just in time and Erin froze. She had nowhere to hide, and running would just get her lost.

Her fists flexed with the need to fight. She was fast and feisty. She could handle four guys, if she was estimating right by the sounds of their voices.

Give her a rifle and this would be over in seven seconds.

But Erin's only weapon was herself and surprise, and she wouldn't give that up so easily.

She sneaked forward, crouching low so she

wouldn't be in anyone's line of sight, and took in the situation. Just as estimated, four men sat around a card table, one with his legs propped up on it. He wore a shoulder holster.

There was a machine gun on the table right next to something that might have been a sheathed knife, but strangely narrow.

She was pretty sure regular crew didn't go around armed to the gills.

She wasn't fast enough to take out both guns before one of those guys scooped up the machine gun and cut her down.

Erin backed up, and the walkway under her feet creaked. She didn't pause. The ship was a noisy beast, and there was no way they could know she was right there.

They shouldn't have, anyway. But their chatter stopped, and then she heard them move.

Erin ran.

"Freeze."

She should have ignored the word. She *wanted* to ignore it. There was no reason to abide. But her body was gripped by the impossible to resist demand and Erin stood still.

"Turn around."

Again, through no volition of her own, she

turned.

The four men stood at the mouth of the hallway. One was unarmed. Two bore guns. And one held the weird wooden thing she'd thought was a knife.

He grinned, and her stomach curdled. "Good try, girl." He waved the stick around and Erin spotted engravings she couldn't quite make sense of. And was it sparkling? She couldn't even narrow her eyes for a better look. "But you're not escaping that easily. Sleep."

She collapsed to the floor.

## CHAPTER TWO

Jericho Gibson couldn't stop pacing. His boots thudded against the concrete floor of the Brooklyn office, each step echoing down the corridor. He wanted to growl, needed to run. Anything to get rid of the aching hole in his chest. Jackson was gone, had been taken a week ago. And they were no closer to finding her. Every trail was cold, every lead exhausted.

She might already be dead.

"Hey." Owen's voice grated against Gibson's temper. Owen had a damned smile on his face. It was a cautious one, but Gibson still wanted to use his claws and swipe it away. "We'll find her," the smiling nuisance said. "Hell, knowing Jackson, she's probably escaped already and blown something up just to prove she could."

Gibson halted mid-step, his jaw clenched as he stared at the cracked white paint on the walls. Owen was trying to help, and that was why Gibson didn't do more than glare. He couldn't shake the visions of Jackson bound and terrified. Or worse.

"Don't you have a mate to annoy?" It was taking all of Gibson's considerable restraint to stop himself from shoving Owen aside.

The cautious smile slipped from Owen's face and transformed into a glare. "We all care about Jackson."

Gibson didn't know how to respond to that. Of course they did. She was an integral part of their group—their pack. And if Gibson had to choose any one of them to have at his back, it would be Erin Jackson. She was the kind of woman that exuded cool competence.

That was *all* she could be.

Gibson refused to show favorites, and his pack was both his business and his family. She worked for him. She was more than a decade younger than him, and he'd been an officer while she was enlisted.

All those reasons didn't mean he could stop caring.

"I know that." Gibson forced himself to take a deep breath. Emotion threatened to overwhelm him, and that made him useless.

Owen sighed. He raised a hand as if he was about to clasp Gibson's shoulder, but lost his nerve and let the hand drop. "We'll find her, and we'll bring her home."

"Of course." He had to stay cool. Calm. He'd keep it together. For the pack.

For Jackson.

"Damn straight," Owen said, that persistent smile back on his face.

"Go get some damn work done," Gibson said. This much talking already had him on edge. If Owen said another word, Gibson would not hold himself responsible for what he did next.

Owen laughed and headed into the main room down the hall, where Bryan Vega was poring over every bit of data they had that might lead them back to Jackson.

Gibson slammed his fist against the wall, squeezing his eyes shut as he was assaulted by the possibilities of what might be happening to Jackson. She was a strong soldier, a resilient woman, and when she got angry, she had a mouth on her.

A mouth he wasn't allowed to think about.

Gibson had spent the better part of the last three years not thinking of Erin Jackson's mouth. Or her curves. Or the little sound she made every time she ate one of those small disks of cheese wrapped in red wax he made sure to keep stocked in the fridge.

He cared for every single member of his team. If any one of them was taken, he'd move heaven and earth to get them back. He *had* done that to rescue Owen, and then Bryan's mate, Kerry. The impossible sense of responsibility would have crushed another man, but Gibson carried the mantle.

But he knew he wasn't reacting the same to Jackson's abduction as he would to anyone else. She was different. Even if he never said a word, never gave a *hint* of it, she was...

She couldn't be his.

That didn't matter right now. Not when he had to bring her home.

He entered the main room to find Owen, Owen's mate Stasia, and Bryan huddled around a table and examining the papers piled in front of them. Owen had set his giant drink cup right at the edge of their work space.

"Move that fucking cup, Owen!" Gibson grunted, reaching past the man to grab it himself. It was mostly ice and he chucked it in the garbage. "Don't spill your shit over the papers."

The tension in the room grew thick as his pack exchanged uneasy glances, and that only made Gibson want to growl. His wolf was a caged beast inside of him. He needed to get out of here.

"Enough!" Stasia was the one brave enough to speak. She glared at him the same way she must have glared at interns back when she was an ER doctor. "I don't appreciate your tone with my mate, or with any of us. We're doing the best we can. The others have been working day and night, too. I think Vi's just about exhausted her magic trying to scry."

Gibson clenched his fists before his emotions could get the better of him. His people needed a leader, not a hothead. Jackson needed him.

Feeling a bit stupid, Gibson grabbed the cup from the trash and set it on the counter. "I'm sorry."

Owen shrugged, but Stasia still looked at him cautiously.

"Do we have any new leads?" Gibson asked.

Bryan shook his head. "Rowe said Vi is going to try another spell with her coven, but I haven't heard from them in a few hours."

"Follow up." The familiar comfort of routine orders did more than any words could to ease

Gibson's worry. "If Vi needs materials, we'll pay. And I'll call in any favor if she needs more."

"Got it, boss." Bryan pulled his phone out of his pocket before he left the room to make the call.

Gibson took his spot at the table. "Walk me through it again," he told Owen. "What are we missing?"

# CHAPTER THREE

Erin woke in a smaller room this time. Her hands were bound by ropes instead of handcuffs. But the cold steel of the chair underneath her wouldn't budge, no matter how hard she struggled. And the salt air that tickled her nose was an unfriendly reminder that she was far from home.

She'd been so close. And she really wished she was back in a world where she didn't know magic existed.

That was a useless thought. She couldn't waste her time on it. Whoever was keeping her captive had some sort of magic wand or whatever that they could use to control her.

That meant that she had to make sure that when

she escaped this time—and she was going to escape —no one saw her.

Easier said than done.

In the back of her mind, she wondered what they planned to do with her. Torture was obvious, but she'd been held for some time and no one had laid a finger on her. She'd been fed, and they must have done something to her—maybe used the magic wand thing—because she didn't have to pee. But that curiosity wouldn't do her any good. She wasn't going to sit in dread and wonder what they wanted from her. She was going to take herself out of the equation.

Somehow.

Erin struggled against the rope and bit back a sound of triumph as it gave just a little. A little led to a lot. And within a few minutes, she was able to slip her hand free, wincing with every inch of move- ment. She was raw, bloodied. But she was out.

Whoever had tied her bonds was no sailor. Or at least not one with any experience in tying rope. Her feet were tied a bit better, but with her hands free, getting loose only took a bit more struggle and wiggling.

For a brief second, Erin consider shifting into her other form. Maybe if she had claws and teeth, it wouldn't be so easy to take her down. But she decided against it. Opposable thumbs were way more important than claws.

The door to the room she was stuck in was locked. Of course. Whoever was holding her wasn't completely incompetent and wouldn't make the same mistakes twice. Erin didn't want to slam into the door and summon extra guards, but she didn't have another choice. No matter how hard she hit it, the door didn't budge.

Erin slumped back against the wall and squinted at the brightness in the room.

Where was the light coming from?

There was no light fixture above her head. But on the other side of the room, she spotted a window.

She ran for it and peered out, disappointed to see that it didn't lead straight to the ocean, but instead to some other interior room of the ship. On the bright side, that meant this window opened. And it wasn't secured nearly as well as the door. With a bit of maneuvering, Erin was able to slip through.

Now she just had to find a way off the ship.

Gibson was going to kill her when she got back. Or at least ream her out.

She could imagine the way his eyes would flash

in that forbidding look he had. She was pretty sure he had made lesser grunts cry back in his active-duty days.

There was only one kind of way she wanted him to make her cry out.

No. She couldn't think about that. She didn't let herself. Now even more than normal.

But what she wouldn't give for his strong arms holding her right now, keeping her warm, encouraging her to keep moving.

The voice of his that she only let herself imagine in her darkest dreams was exactly what she needed. She could almost hear him in her thoughts.

But hallucinating a savior wasn't going to get her off the ship. And Erin didn't need a savior. She could save herself.

A sexy, gruff, older cheerleader with bright blue eyes and a way of looking at her that made her want to melt, on the other hand... No. She didn't get to fantasize about Jericho Gibson. Erin turned her mind to the task.

Wherever she was, it wasn't New York. And even though she had no doubt that Gibson was looking for her, just as he would look for any other member of their pack, he had no way to know she was here. Wherever *here* was. She had to get out of this floating prison and find a phone so she could go home to him.

Erin thought she heard someone coming down the corridor door and froze for a second before slipping back into a small alcove. After a few seconds, no one came close, and it might have just been the moaning and groaning noises of the ship.

At the very edge of the large room she was in, she found a door labeled emergency exit. Well. This was an emergency and she needed exit. She was worried a bit about an alarm sounding, but it was a risk she had to take. Eventually someone would notice she wasn't tied to that chair anymore.

Erin slammed through the open door and cursed as she almost pitched over a railing and into the swirling ocean below.

She was on the lower part of the ship, maybe twenty feet above the water.

Erin didn't let herself think. They were in some kind of port. The water had to be deep enough for the ship. She could swim.

She threw herself over the edge and crashed into the churning, grimy water of the port. The frigid water stole the breath from her lungs, and her whole body threatened to seize up. But Erin had been trained for this. Years in the military—though this was a reminder of why she had joined the Army rather than the Navy—and swimming at the gym whenever she got the chance.

She let her body sink into motion, arms moving steadily, legs kicking. Cold was a problem for later. She couldn't catch hypothermia if she kept moving. Something was off about that, but wasting time to think would only make her colder.

Slowly, agonizingly slowly, she got closer to shore. Eventually she managed to swim between two ships in a move that was no doubt incredibly dangerous. She found a ladder that took her out of the gross, dirty water of the port and onto dry land.

The sun was high in the sky, but no one was around. Erin shivered in place for just a moment, wringing as much water out of her hair and her top as she could manage.

Now that she was standing still, the bloody skin on her wrists hurt even more, but that was another thing she wasn't wasting time worrying about. Pain was a problem for later.

She had to keep moving.

Erin did her best to keep out of sight. She was in some kind of industrial port, no doubt in a restricted area. The mere fact that she was soaking wet would draw attention. The fact that she had no ID and wasn't eager to tell her story might cause problems.

Erin managed to slip past the gate and make it to a public parking lot. Behind her, she saw a sign for the Port of Norfolk, Virginia.

Definitely a long way from home.

She had no phone. No money. And if her clothes didn't dry soon, she might catch her death. All she knew was that New York was north and vaguely east of Virginia. Changing into her other form and running hundreds of miles as a wolf wasn't an option. A wolf couldn't carry a map.

And four wheels were way faster than four legs.

Erin's eyes slipped over all of the cars in the lot, an idea already forming. She dismissed everything that looked like it might have been produced in the last ten years. Too much tech, too big of an opportunity for anti-theft features.

But the beat up twenty-year-old sedan nestled in between two large SUVs might just do the trick.

Erin wasn't a thief. She felt kind of bad for what she was about to do. But she had to put distance between herself and her captors. They would figure out she was gone soon. She wasn't letting them put her back on that ship.

She tested the handle on the door and figured it was fate when the vehicle opened.

No lock? Basically asking to get stolen.

She was still shivering in her wet clothes, and the driver's seat was covered in badly stained cloth that smelled faintly of old cigarettes and weed.

The back of the car was stuffed full of clothing, like somebody heading home from a semester at college. The timing didn't quite work out and Erin hated to make this person's day any worse, but she had needs.

She dug through clothes quickly, thankful that they smelled clean, and pulled out a pair of sweats and a shirt that would do the trick. She didn't bother stealing a pair of underwear and there were no bras. An ancient pair of sandals was about three sizes too big, but she tightened the straps as much as she could and called it good enough.

It was fine. For the moment.

Hotwiring the car took only a minute, and Erin pulled out onto the street and chose a direction at random.

She drove for about fifteen minutes, headed towards the city but unsure of what else to do. She needed to get in touch with Gibson, to let him know she was okay. But the car only had a quarter tank of gas and eventually someone would be looking for it.

Did this person have a cell phone in their car? Not likely. But at a red light, Erin reached over and opened the glove box in hope. A white envelope fell out and spilled a few twenties onto the floor.

Erin grinned and started to believe that some god of luck was smiling down on her.

At the next light, she counted the cash. It might be enough to make it back to New York between gas and some food, but the more she stopped, the more likely she was to get caught.

Besides, she felt bad enough about stealing the car that she didn't want to take it out of state. If she ditched it in the city, there was a decent chance it would be returned to its rightful owner, sans a little cash and some clothes.

Decision made, Erin found a different parking lot and pulled in. She was careful to wipe down as much of the interior of the vehicle as she could and hoped she didn't leave too much DNA evidence.

With cash in hand, she walked several blocks until she found a 24-hour diner that looked like it catered to a rougher crowd.

The waitress took one look at Erin's pilfered clothes, and the sandals that flapped against the tile despite tightening the straps to the breaking point. Erin flashed her cash. It wasn't much, but it was enough to let the lady know that she could pay for a meal.

"Can I use your phone?" Erin asked the woman, letting some of her exhaustion seep into her voice. "I had a really bad day."

The waitress shrugged, lips pursed and attitude aloof. "As long as you buy something afterwards, go for it."

———

The walls of Gibson's apartment were starting to close in on him. He needed to run, but there were few places in the city good enough to be really satisfying. And if he headed back to the office, he knew he'd face a mutiny. His pack said he needed to rest.

As if he could rest before Jackson was back safe with him.

With all of them.

The annoying ring of his cell phone was enough to make him growl, and he didn't recognize the number, but with so many feelers out he couldn't ignore a call, no matter his mood.

"What?" he barked, grip on the phone strong enough that he distantly worried he'd crack it.

Someone breathed into the other end of the line, and there was a faint sound of clinking and murmured voices in the background. "Who is this?" he demanded.

The person on the other end of the line sucked in a deep breath. "Gibson. It's me."

Erin.

Jackson.

A sound ripped out of Gibson from somewhere he buried deep, the growing fear that Jackson wasn't coming back ripped away as if the worry had never been there.

"Jackson? Where the hell are you? What's your status?" There was a struggle to keep his voice professional, to hide the anguish that tore him to bits. She was one of his people, and he had to be strong. He had to be exactly the same leader for her as he would for anyone else.

Her breathing evened, and the sounds in the background faded. When she spoke, it was crisp, clear. "Norfolk, Virginia. They had me on a ship and I just got out. I'm in some random diner I found. I dumped the car, but there was a bit of cash that I took. I don't think I should drive it all the way up to New York."

The words came out fast and jumped around, but Gibson kept up. She'd escaped and stolen a car. Maybe she was a bit guilty about that. He didn't give a single damn about the car. Not if it meant that Jackson was safe.

His mind started churning, the sluggishness from days without sleep sloughing off now that Jackson was so close, even if she was four states away. "How much money?"

She paused for a moment, and he heard the scratch of paper. "About a hundred bucks."

"Hold on." Gibson pulled his phone away from his ear, careful not to drop the call, and did a quick search of the phone number Erin was calling from. She was in a tiny diner in the center of Norfolk. He looked up more information and then put the phone back to his ear, his path more clear than it had been in days. "I'm coming to get you. I want you to go to the Ocean View Sleep Inn and get a room." He gave her the address. "I'll be there as soon as I can." More words perched on the tip of his tongue, threatening to trip out. He couldn't say them over the phone.

Or ever.

Jackson let out a whoosh of breath, and he could

almost see the faint smile tugging at the side of her mouth. "Got it. I'll be waiting." They ended the call.

He didn't bother to pack a bag. He summoned a car from his phone and started looking up flights. There were plenty heading to Virginia, but the soonest flight cost over a thousand dollars. If he was willing to wait another hour, he'd save hundreds.

But that was another hour that Jackson would be alone and friendless, with enemies searching for her in every corner of the city.

Gibson bought the expensive flight and made it through security and onto the plane with only minutes to spare.

Only after take off did he realize that he hadn't told anyone else in the pack about Jackson's call. He should have, he knew that. They lived in a world of danger and magic and plenty of trouble, and he was the boss of it all. He couldn't just hie off to play the hero at a moment's notice.

But with Jackson's voice still fresh in his mind, he couldn't bring himself to care.

Once they were in the air, he paid the eight dollars to purchase wi-fi and sent an email to Myers. Owen couldn't keep his mouth shut and would tell the others that in just a few hours, Gibson and Jackson would be heading home.

The rest of the flight was a blur.

On the ground in Virginia and in another summoned car, this one going to the motel he had told Erin to book, Gibson tapped his hand impatiently against his leg. It had been more than three hours since the call. His mind summoned up every horrible scenario he could imagine: the room splashed with blood, Jackson back in her captor's hands.

Or worse.

He curled his hands into fists and scowled. He had to keep it together. He knew where she was supposed to be, and she'd spent a lot of years taking care of herself.

As soon as he was with her, he would keep her safe.

But as the car pulled into the motel, Gibson realized he didn't know her room number. She didn't have a phone with her, so she couldn't call to leave him a message.

It didn't matter. He would bang on every door in the motel until he found her, if that was what it took. Or he would ask at the reception desk.

It wasn't necessary. He passed the room on the farthest corner and saw a familiar blonde figure sitting in a chair and flipping through channels on the TV.

Gibson stood frozen and stared for a moment.

She was there.

She was safe.

Heart thundering in his chest, he crossed to her door and knocked. His fingers shook just a little, but he didn't care. There was a sheen of sweat on his palm. He couldn't quite pull in a deep enough breath.

The TV turned off. And a moment later, she unlocked the door and opened it.

There stood Erin Jackson. Worse for wear in sweats that were too big for her, hair damp from the shower, wrists bandaged, with angry red skin peeking out, and a nasty bruise under one of her eyes.

But she was alive.

And she was looking at him with the same quiet desperation that he knew was reflected on his own face.

He needed to say something. Needed to step back. Needed to get them into a car and headed home.

Instead, Gibson stepped forward and kissed her.

# CHAPTER FOUR

Gɪʙsᴏɴ's ᴄᴀʟʟᴏᴜsᴇᴅ hand cradled the nape of Erin's neck, his thumb tracing the curve of her jaw. This shouldn't be happening, but Erin couldn't pull away. The kiss made her shiver, but not with cold. She was burning up from the inside out, her body arching against the one man she couldn't touch.

But his mouth was moving over hers, each stroke of his tongue a slow, deliberate dance that left her aching for more.

Gibson pulled her closer, wrapping his arms around her waist while she wound her fingers through his thick, wavy hair. Erin wanted to melt against him, let herself be swept away in this moment.

After the last days, the confusion, the escape, she'd earned this.

Hadn't she?

"More," she breathed against his lips, when it seemed like he was pulling away. One of them was supposed to be strong here.

"Erin..." he groaned, and the sound of her first name on his tongue was too much. They were always so careful.

But not right now.

The world outside might have already ended, Erin couldn't tell, not when she was too wrapped up in the taste of Gibson, the feel of his body.

"Jericho," she whispered against his lips, the name feeling forbidden. He jerked against her, but only tightened his grip.

Her entire being was consumed by the storm that raged between them. For once, she let herself give in. She needed this. Needed him.

"Jericho," she whispered again. Speaking any louder might break the spell that had them both enraptured. Her fingers found the hem of his shirt and began to pull it upward.

Erin's breath caught as she took in the sight of Gibson's bare chest, his muscular frame a testament to the strength and power he wielded. The scars that adorned his body told a story of battles fought and survived, and they only made her want him more.

He wasn't young, and it showed in the hint of gray in his chest hair, and in some of the roughened red skin that she'd never see on a younger man. But the patina of experience only made him sexier.

With a sudden growl, Gibson scooped her up into his arms, cradling her against his chest and striding toward the bed.

He lay Erin down and her heart pounded. Gibson towered over her, standing at her feet like some conquering hero—or a ravaging wolf. And she wanted him to ravage her, so much that her entire body was slick with need. All of that just from a kiss, a look.

She was in so much trouble.

She'd never felt this exposed before. No one else could strip her down to nothing with a single glance and still make her want to take away more. Her emotions were laid out for him and only for him. There was no hiding from this. Not now.

Gibson's hands gripped the waistband of her sweats, his eyes locked onto hers as he slowly pulled them down her legs. The sensation of the fabric sliding against her skin sent shivers down her spine. She could feel the scrape of his fingers even through the soft fabric and couldn't wait until he was touching her bare skin.

As her sweat pooled at her feet, she knew there was no turning back. There'd been no chance of that, not since the moment their lips touched.

Erin's breath hitched when Gibson knelt before her, his strong hands gently spreading her thighs apart. She'd never dared to imagine this, no matter how deeply she wanted. Gibson held her soul in his hands, and he could crush her into nothing.

He wouldn't, though. She was more certain of that than anything else.

*Mate.*

The forbidden word whispered through her mind as his warm breath ghosted over her sensitive skin, causing goosebumps to rise along her body. Erin bit her lip, trying to hold back the whimper that threatened to escape her mouth.

The first touch of Gibson's lips against her sex sent a shockwave through her. Her fingers clutched the bed sheets, knuckles turning white from the intensity of her grip. He spread her out like a starving man at a feast, and she couldn't deny him.

"Jericho," she whispered, her voice barely audible and still reveling in this secret moment where he could be hers as sensation threatened to consume her.

Gibson's eyes flicked up, dark with desire and something deeper—that connection both of them had felt for years and yet couldn't acknowledge.

As Gibson's—Jericho's—tongue danced along her folds, exploring and teasing, Erin's body trembled with anticipation. His focus was solely on her pleasure, as if nothing else existed in that moment.

———

The taste of Erin Jackson was going to kill him. And Gibson could die a happy man. But not a satisfied one, not until he knew what this woman, *his* woman, looked like as she came apart in ecstasy.

While his mouth continued to drive Erin closer and closer to that edge, he could no longer ignore the throbbing need between his legs. His cock strained against his jeans, a pulsing reminder of what he needed.

With one last lingering kiss on her sex, Gibson shifted back onto his knees and quickly shucked off his pants. His cock sprang free, hard and dripping with need. Erin's gaze was riveted to the sight, her breathing growing shallow.

"Touch yourself," she whispered, the words sending a shock wave through him.

Gibson gripped his cock, eyes glued to her as he began to stroke, slowly at first, then with increasing urgency. He'd always prided himself on his restraint, his control. But he was helpless at Erin's feet, her taste on his tongue and her eyes holding him transfixed.

Anything she wanted was hers. *He* was hers. If only she would ask.

Every second in all the years they'd known each other was leading to this moment, the air crackling with desire. If Gibson had any strength, he would have pulled back before they crossed a final line, something that couldn't be undone. But this dingy motel was a place out of time, something that they couldn't walk away from.

His chest tightened with emotion. He wanted to say something, but words failed him.

As Gibson stroked himself, Erin reached down and let her fingers play over her sex. "Please," she whispered, "I need you."

The raw vulnerability and desire in Erin's voice made him feel powerful, yet achingly tender. He couldn't deny her—not this, not now. Not when he ached just as much as she did.

He said something hoarsely, maybe her name, maybe a prayer, as he crawled up onto the bed and over her body, positioning himself between her legs. Her eyes were lidded in arousal, watching his every move with undisguised want.

She reached out to guide him closer and wrapped her legs around his waist, pulling him near until the tip of his cock pressed against her entrance.

He searched her eyes for any sign of doubt, but there wasn't a hint of hesitation, not in this stolen moment outside of reality where they could come together not as Gibson and Jackson, with all the obstacles that kept them apart in the real world, but as Jericho and Erin, their true selves.

Gibson slid into her, her wet heat enveloping him. He groaned against the perfect fit of it, the thing he'd been denying for so long just as exhilarating as he'd imagined.

Erin cried out as her climax built, her fingers digging into his shoulders. Her voice was filled with passion and something deeper still, a connection that he couldn't let himself dream of.

He couldn't hold back any longer as her body rippled around him. He buried his face in her neck, breathing in the scent of her sweat and sex.

As they trembled in each other's arms, spent and

sated, Gibson couldn't suppress the nagging thought that tried to whisper doubts into the back of his mind. It felt so perfect to be wrapped up in Erin's arms, the fabric of her t-shirt scratchy against his skin.

His pants still clung to one of his ankles. She hadn't taken off her shirt. They'd both been so wrapped up in the reality of touching one another that they hadn't taken a second to fully appreciate it and revel in their nakedness.

It was the nakedness of his emotions he couldn't hide. Beside him Erin was flushed, eyes bright and sated. But even now he could see the wariness creeping in, the emotional walls that always stood tall between them being rebuilt brick by brick.

He wanted to smash through them, demand that she acknowledge what they were, a word that he couldn't even *think*, let alone say.

Instead of saying anything, he pulled her close and breathed in her scent until it settled something deep inside him.

He didn't know how to keep her, but he couldn't make himself let her go.

# CHAPTER FIVE

REALITY SEEPED into Erin right along with the heat from Gibson's body where it pressed up against hers. Her shirt had rucked up while they slept, exposing half her back, and she still wasn't wearing sweats. Her body ached in a satisfying reminder of what she'd done.

Her mind, though? The ache there wasn't satisfying.

She'd just had sex with Jericho Gibson.

Her boss. An officer. The leader of her pack.

Fuck.

Could they uncross the line they'd barreled over in a mix of heated kisses and burning caresses? The raw emotion of it all had torn her open until there was nothing left. Knowing it was a mistake was salt in the wound. Life back in New York didn't have room for them as anything more than co-workers. Adding romance to the mix... or whatever this was... would only disrupt their cohesion.

*You know what this is*, some secret part buried deep inside of her whispered. Right along with that word she didn't dare to think.

*Mate.*

Gibson stirred beside her, his eyes opening just enough to reveal the deep blue irises that reminded her of moonlit runs through dense forests. He blinked at her for a second, sleep clouding his eyes, until he realized he was still holding onto her, his cock brushing up against her ass.

Without a word, Gibson rolled over and threw the covers aside to stand up, leaving her exposed. The AC chilled air hit her skin, and Erin pulled the sheets up to cover herself, watching as Gibson padded towards the bathroom.

The silence hurt, even if it was for the best. And it wasn't like she was saying anything either. Where could she even start?

Gibson half-turned back toward her. "Jackson..." he trailed off, as if unsure how to continue, before shaking his head and going into the bathroom, shutting the door behind him.

Jackson. Not Erin.

"Right," she whispered, swallowing past the lump in her throat. "Got it, boss."

The sound of water splashing against the sink echoed past the door, and Erin forced herself to get up, even if she was shivering in the chilly room. She snatched her pilfered sweats from where they'd fallen on the floor and pulled them on. The cotton was flimsy armor against what she really wanted, but it was all she had at the moment.

Gibson shut the water off, and Erin took a steadying breath. Once he was out of that bathroom, she had to be his loyal soldier, not his... whatever she couldn't be. She just needed another minute.

Or another decade in his bed.

Erin smoothed a hand down her wrinkled shirt as Gibson exited the bathroom, his face the neutral calm he normally exuded. But there was a tension in his jaw that wasn't normally there, and a set to his shoulders that told her his calm was little more than a facade.

"Everyone will be relieved that you're back," he said, avoiding looking at her as he picked up his shirt from the chair. "Owen was going crazy without you."

"Only Owen?" She regretted the words as they

came out. Especially when Gibson looked away from her, as if looking her in the eye would admit too much.

She winced as she rubbed a finger against her wrist. Gibson noticed and stared at the healing red wounds—a stark reminder of the handcuff and ropes that had torn her skin bloody. His eyes darkened. "How are those healing?" The same question she knew he'd ask any of their packmates. But there was an underlying rage to the question.

"Fine," she replied, forcing herself to stop poking at her wounds. "Nothing I can't handle."

"Once we're back home, I want Stasia to check you out. Back in New York," he clarified, as he if thought she might mistake his meaning. As if they might truly be going *home* together.

"Home, right. How are we getting back? I don't exactly have ID to get on a plane." She wasn't sure how long a car ride might be, and she didn't relish hours in a small vehicle with only Gibson and the things they weren't saying.

"I can get you on the plane, I just need to call a friend at the TSA." That was the Gibson she knew and... respected. He seemed to have a friend in every agency and precinct in the country.

Gibson patted his pants and stuck his hand in the

pocket before pulling it out, then he looked over at the nightstand. "Have you seen my phone? Or my wallet?"

Erin glanced around the room, but all the surfaces were clear. "Maybe they fell?" Erin crouched down beside the bed to look and hoped she didn't see any of the gross surprises that might be waiting under a motel room bed.

There was nothing.

She stood back up. "Did you bring a jacket?" Erin asked, but she didn't remember peeling one off of him in their mad scramble for the bed.

Gibson shoved the mattress aside in an impressive show of strength, but all that revealed were some dust bunnies and a stain she didn't want to think about. He marched back into the bathroom and then stomped out empty handed.

"We would have heard if someone came in here," he said.

Erin agreed.

"Keep looking," he commanded, as if Erin had stopped.

But there was no sign of his stuff.

Erin had the sneaking suspicion that this was some kind of magic bullshit. Wallets and phones didn't just disappear. "I'll call the front office and see if anyone turned your stuff in." Her hand hovered over the beige receiver.

"I'd know if I dropped my phone outside," Gibson snapped. He flipped a small chair to its side to look under it a second time.

Erin glared. If he wanted to be an ass, she'd hit him right back. "Because you were paying so much attention when you stepped into the room." Her temper matched his, getting worse by the second. Erin wanted to go *home*. She wanted to curl up in her own bed and lick her wounds, to harden her heart until there wasn't the tiniest crack left for Jericho Gibson to sneak through.

He blushed. Like really, actually blushed. And Erin felt her own cheeks heat in response. Gibson went back to searching, and Erin picked up the phone. Nothing but silence greeted her.

Strange.

She pressed the button in the phone cradle a couple of times, but she didn't get a dial tone.

"Weird." She carefully put the phone back down and stared at it for a second.

"What's weird?" Gibson gave up on his search and crossed his arms.

"The phone isn't working. Not even to call the

front desk." She picked it up again, as if it might magically decide to function.

"Did you try pressing the lever a few times?" he asked, taking a step closer as if he might yank the phone out of her hands. "It's not like a cell phone."

"I'm twenty-seven, Major. I know how to use a phone. Or did you want me to try again and see if we can get the operator on the line, like you had to do when you were a kid?" Erin might have bit her tongue before, but a whole week of captivity and then the aftermath of it all was catching up to her.

"I was born in the eighties," Gibson said, strangely defensive.

"The eighteen-eighties?"

"Did you body swap with Owen in the last ten minutes? You don't usually talk like this, Jackson." But there was a hint of a smile in the snap.

Erin tried the phone one last time and slapped it down with more force than necessary when it didn't work. She made sure the cord was plugged into the wall and scowled when she saw it was.

"What if it's magic?" she asked, bile rising in her throat. She remembered the device her captor had used on her, the way she couldn't even begin to fight it. What if...

"It's a cheap-ass motel," Gibson reminded her,

as if she wasn't the one on her knees breathing in nasty air. "Phone's probably just a dud."

Erin got back up and wiped as much dust off as she could. "Yeah, I hope." Her shoulder itched and she rolled it around to try and work out the sensation. It faded.

Gibson noticed. "What's the matter?"

What wasn't?

She didn't want to think about her time on the boat, but Gibson needed the information. "The people who were holding me, there were at least four of them that I saw. One of them had this magic device. He held it up in front of me and told me to sleep and I just passed out. There was nothing to resist, it was just *boom* and I was out. Sort of like what Vega described when we got Owen back." She hadn't thought of it at the time, but her packmate, Owen, had recently been taken by hostile forces, and they'd learned about that nasty little magic trick while rescuing him.

Gibson didn't say anything, but his expression was stormy.

Erin let herself think it out. "There has to be some sort of limitation on it. Otherwise they could have just told me not to escape."

"Sounds like." His tone was cautious.

"I'm really getting sick of this magic stuff." It was one thing to be a shifter, the rest of it Erin could do without.

"Me too."

"Maybe I'm going crazy, but it feels like something weird is going on. Let's give the room another look, search for anything magicky that might be screwing with us." The thought was nagging at her. "All I brought with me are the clothes on my back and those sandals, and I got all of that from the car I stole. But I've seen some of the stuff that Vi can do and I don't think it's outside the realm of possibility that a witch could, I don't know, transport something here." Vi was the pack's resident witch, and the mate of Rowe. Her powers could be scary at times, and Erin was happy she was one of the good guys.

If Gibson thought she was crazy, he didn't say. He turned and started looking.

Erin wasn't sure what she was looking for, exactly, but she started under the bed. And a minute later, her fingers ran over a tear in the carpet that abutted the wall. Then she felt a strange flatness. Erin carefully extracted it and stared at the thin, wand-like device.

It sort of looked like a stick, but it felt too

smooth to be real wood. There were deep, dark grooves in the material and a strange purplish color at one tip. It even seemed to shimmer in the light. But was it magic?

"I think I found something." Her voice didn't shake when she said it, thankfully. She didn't want Gibson to know how much this all spooked her.

Gibson reached out and took the object from Erin's hand, studying it carefully. His brow furrowed. Then a hint of recognition flickered in his eyes, followed by a smile that made Erin's stomach flip.

"This isn't magical," Gibson said. "Not unless High Sorceress Serafina De Fantasia is actually real. My niece loves that show, and she has the toy this came with. It's attached to Serafina and falls off really easily. It's just plastic."

"Your niece?" That was a shock, but she didn't know why. "I didn't know you had a niece." Gibson was the kind of guy who seemed to have sprung from stone. She didn't think of him as having a family.

He ran a hand through his hair, and shrugged. "Yeah," he admitted, clearing his throat. "I have a younger sister. Her daughter, Bee, is six. Sorceress

Serafina was the guest of honor at our last tea party."

Erin tried to picture the reserved, serious Jericho Gibson playing with a giggling little girl, and couldn't do it until suddenly she could. And that hurt even more.

What would he be like with kids of his own?

She wasn't going down that road.

"Let's ask the office about your wallet and phone. Maybe you really did drop them." But somehow she doubted it.

Erin had a bit of cash left—provided it hadn't also been magicked away—but she had no idea how she and Gibson were going to get home.

# CHAPTER SIX

It was offensively sunny and bright. A cool mist blew off the ocean, making the day feel even more pleasant. Gibson didn't like it. And he almost smiled when he looked down at the cracked pavement of the sidewalk leading from their room to the motel office and noticed crinkled and abandoned fast food wrappers and crushed soda cans.

The motel was right on the beach, but given the cost per night of a room, cleanliness was not the top priority.

A man, possibly another guest, leaned against a beat up old pickup truck and smoked a cigarette. His eyes followed Jackson, and his lips pulled into a nasty grin as she walked right by him.

Jealousy surged, his wolf growling deep inside of

him, and Gibson was tempted to stride forward and take the man by the throat, letting his fingers curl tight until they left bruises against pale skin.

Jackson was a few steps ahead of him and Gibson cursed himself. He had no right to those thoughts. She wasn't his. And the man was just looking, even if he was a creep. He didn't say anything.

The door creaked ominously as Jackson opened it and entered the motel office. Gibson followed right after, schooling his face into the same neutral expression he'd learned to use when superior officers said incredibly stupid things.

A young man, no more than twenty-five, sat behind the counter, and he grinned when he saw Jackson.

Gibson's wolf tried to do something again, bare his teeth, flash his claws. It was immature. He was better than this. And if he didn't get control of himself, Jackson would kick his ass.

He would deserve it.

"What's up?" asked the clerk. "Was everything all right with your room?"

Jackson leaned one elbow against the beat up old desk, a strange smile on her face.

Gibson couldn't deal. He stepped forward,

ending up just a little bit too close to her, but he didn't move. Frankly, it was a miracle he didn't sling an arm over her shoulders and growl at the clerk that Jackson was his.

"I'm looking for my phone and my wallet," said Gibson, trying to keep his voice neutral. "We were searching in the room this morning, but we couldn't find them. Thought maybe someone might have turned them in."

The clerk gave them both a doubtful look. "Was it expensive? Because I doubt anyone would turn that in."

"Do you have a lost and found?" Gibson asked, teeth set in a rictus of a grin.

The clerk shrugged. "I'll check."

He came back a second later with a neon green wallet that had an illustrated image of a turtle on it. "Is this it?" he asked, sarcasm dripping from his voice. "There's a coupon for the pizza place down the street and a certificate from Shady Hill Elementary School for perfect attendance in the fourth grade. Is that your wallet?"

This time, Gibson did growl. Jackson stepped in for him. "I don't think so," she said, placing a hand on his arm to keep him from doing anything. "Thanks for checking." She paused. "Would it be possible for me to use your phone?" Her voice was brusquely professional.

It should have made Gibson feel better. She wasn't encouraging the guy. She was a beautiful woman. People were going to look at her. He didn't get to say shit about that.

The clerk gave them a legitimately apologetic look and then pointed at the ancient desktop in front of him. "We use this computer-phone thing," he said, struggling to explain it. "There's not like a phone you can just dial. I can't let you borrow it. I'm sorry. But there's a diner right across the street. They do a cheap breakfast and I bet they'd let you use the phone."

Frustration erupted, and Gibson turned on a heel and stormed out of the office, Jackson hot on his heels.

"What was that about?" Jackson demanded as they crossed the cracked pavement of the parking lot. The guy by the truck smoking a cigarette was long gone, but the scent of his smoke remained.

"It wasn't anything." This was fine. Gibson was a professional, Erin was his employee. No, *Jackson* was his employee. She could be Erin in her off-hours. Erin with other people.

Never Erin with him.

*Liar.*

The thought came from deep within him, that selfish part of his soul that insisted that he knew exactly who Erin Jackson was to him. What she was to him. It whispered a word he refused to name, even as his need to acknowledge it grew stronger and stronger by the second.

They should never have slept together. It was something that he would hold in his memories for the rest of his life, but it couldn't happen again. Especially if it was already messing things up.

The grown up thing to do would be to talk about it.

Gibson didn't really feel like a grown up right now.

"I'm glad we have you back, Jackson," he said, settling into what should have been his old and comfortable role as leader and boss. "It's been a hell of a week."

She gave him a distrusting look, but finally nodded. "It sure beats being held captive."

The diner they walked into could have been anywhere in the country. It smelled of syrup and greasy bacon all overlaid with burnt eggs. Gibson's stomach rumbled. They were led to a table in the back corner, and their waitress delivered coffee to them with the speed of a race car driver.

At the first sip, Gibson's mood started to settle a bit, and once they had food in front of them, his temper cooled. He scarfed down his bacon and eggs, barely taking time to taste them.

Judging by the smile that Jackson threw him, she was feeling a little bit more herself too.

"How did you get to Virginia so fast?" she asked once she set her fork aside. "Yesterday, I mean. It couldn't have been more than three hours after I called you. That seems... I mean did Vi magic you or something?"

"I took the first available flight," he answered. He might regret it once his credit card bill came in, but there wasn't an expense that he wouldn't make to rescue Jackson. What was a thousand bucks compared her safety?

"The first flight? That must have been expensive." She let it hang, not quite a question, but curious.

He shrugged. "It's you."

He should have said that he would have done it for anyone on the team. He should have firmed up the boundary between them. But he knew deep down that if it had been anyone else, he might have waited that hour for the less expensive flight. He at least would have had to think about it.

When it was Jackson, he had handed his credit card over without a second thought.

And judging by the way that Jackson didn't quite meet his eyes, she knew just as well as he did that there was something special about her.

He had to shove it all aside. Erin Jackson wasn't his. He would have to remember their one glorious night together and hold it close for the rest of his life. That was all it could ever be.

———

Erin had to get away from the table. If Gibson started talking again, she might do something crazy, like launch herself at him, start kissing him, and never let him go.

She didn't like his possessive act in the parking lot with that creeper or with the kid behind the motel desk. At least she didn't like it *a lot*. No one had ever been jealous or possessive with her before. She could handle herself. She *had* handled herself for years and years and years, and she liked doing that.

But seeing a guy get a little growly on her

behalf... no, seeing Jericho Gibson get a bit growly on her behalf made her tingle in places she definitely wasn't supposed to be thinking about.

Erin escaped to the front of the diner, where their waitress was cleaning off the counter. "Excuse me," Erin interrupted with a smile. "Can I borrow the diner phone? I'm having a bit of a cell phone issue." It wasn't a lie. Technically. The issue was she didn't have a cell phone with her.

The waitress nodded towards the phone on the counter. "Go for it. Your boyfriend not let you borrow his phone? Kind of a dick move."

Erin choked and had to cough twice to clear her throat. "Not my boyfriend. That's my boss." Something she had been reminding herself of all day, even if her stupid heart and body didn't want to listen.

The waitress glanced back at Gibson and smiled slyly.

Erin's wolf rumbled deep inside her. She didn't like any woman checking out her man.

*Not* her man.

But she still didn't like it. Erin reached for the phone. There was no dial tone. She pulled the receiver away from her ear and stared at it, as if a glare might magically make the dial tone appear. She held the phone back up to her ear. Nothing. She hung it up and picked it back up again and still nothing.

The waitress was staring at her with a questioning look on her face. It gave Erin an idea.

"I have this condition," she said, making it up on the spot. "A metal implant in my wrist. It sometimes interferes with phone signals. Would you mind dialing for me?"

The waitress was skeptical, that much was clear. But the place wasn't busy and she took the phone with a shrug rather than waste time arguing.

Erin gave her Owen's number and felt the first stirrings of excitement as she heard the phone began to ring. They were so close. So, so close. Before anyone answered the phone, the waitress handed the handset over to Erin. She held it up to her ear.

And the call disconnected.

"What the fuck?" It came out way louder than Erin intended, and the few patrons in the diner all looked her way. Erin slammed the phone down and was distantly grateful it didn't break. She wanted to pick it up and smash it until it shattered into a million pieces. It deserved it.

She just wanted to make a damned phone call. Why was that so hard? She raised her hand up, only distantly realizing she was still gripping the handset.

Warm fingers wrapped around her wrist. Familiar fingers. Fingers that had touched her in a much more intimate place.

"Set it down, Erin." Gibson breathed it against her ear.

His body was pressed against her, his muscles warm and hard and so tempting that she wanted to lean back and let him take all of her troubles away.

But they weren't doing that. And they weren't talking about it either.

Erin set the phone down gently and gave the waitress a sheepish smile. The waitress didn't look happy.

Gibson took a moment to settle their bill with the dwindling pile of her cash that luckily had not disappeared, and then they were leaving the diner, still having failed to get in touch with anyone back home.

Once they were outside, Erin's frustration bubbled out of her, and she tipped her head back and screamed before striking out, kicking a crushed soda can clear across the parking lot, where it skittered and spun until it rolled into the road where a passing car crushed it flat.

Erin curled her fingers into fists and clenched so tight that it hurt. She wanted to gouge her fingernails into her palm until they drew blood, but her nails weren't long enough to do that. She wanted to howl, but her throat wouldn't accommodate the sound.

She wanted to go home.

No, she wanted to go back three years to when she was just a normal soldier, not someone mixed up in werewolves and magic and kidnapping and bullshit.

And she wanted to go back twenty minutes ago to before Gibson saw her act out like this. That thought brought her up short.

She was always calm. Always cool. Always collected. When someone needed someone they could count on, they called Erin Jackson. She didn't throw tantrums in beachside parking lots with her boss looking on, a stormy expression on his face.

Erin sucked in a few deep breaths and felt her heart rate start to calm. It was fine. She was fine. She had to be.

Embarrassment washed over her at the fact that Gibson had witnessed her tantrum. But she had to shove that aside. They had seven dollars left and they had to cross half of the eastern seaboard to get home.

When in doubt, turn back to the problem at hand. Erin forced herself to concentrate. "It's a curse. It has to be. Something stopping us from making phone calls and taking our money."

"You were able to call me yesterday," Gibson pointed out. "And your cash didn't disappear."

She had to think about that. Erin wasn't an expert on magic. She wasn't even a novice. But she listened when Vi, the pack's resident witch, spoke, and she tried to put together something that might make sense.

"I had to swim through saltwater to get off the ship," she said, thinking out loud. "I think Vi said something about saltwater disrupting magic. Or maybe they didn't cast a curse on me until someone realized I was gone. It might have taken a while. I kind of snuck away. As for the money, I had that hidden in a plastic bag in the toilet tank. Maybe something about that also disrupted the magic. Or maybe it's because it wasn't in my possession when the curse was cast?" She wasn't sure if it made sense or if Vi would have laughed in her face at the suggestions.

"That doesn't explain my things," Gibson said.

*It's because you're mine.*

Erin had to bite back those words, but something deep in her soul told her they were true. No matter how much she resisted it, no matter how impossible it was, Gibson was hers. Would always be hers. And the magic knew it.

Instead, she shrugged. "I'm not sure. But clearly something happened. Any ideas on how we're going to get home?"

# CHAPTER SEVEN

IT WAS GETTING HOT, the Virginia sun beating down on the parking lot unrelentingly. Erin wished she had a hat. Or a fan. The earlier breeze off the ocean had died down to nothing, and now the only air movement came from cars speeding by too fast, trying to get on the nearby expressway.

Gibson was right behind her, a steady, solid presence she wasn't about to lean into, no matter how much she wanted to. She didn't get to do that. She had to get her brain back on track. Jericho Gibson was her boss. He was the major. Nothing else.

*Mate.*

No. Her brain needed to shut up about that. She didn't get to have him as her mate. They couldn't.

And the sooner they got home, the sooner everything would get back to normal.

"We could shift," Erin suggested, even knowing it was a terrible idea. "We'd cover more ground on four feet." And if she was in her other form, maybe Gibson wouldn't be such a temptation.

Gibson hummed. "It's a long way to go," he said. "And we wouldn't have any clothes if we needed to shift back for some reason."

"And there's probably wolf hunters in Virginia just itching for our pelts." It was half a joke, but Erin realized she might actually be onto something. If they were hiking through the backwoods, there was no telling what dangers they might encounter.

That didn't even start to consider the magical complications.

"Any other ideas? Because a part of me is tempted to dive in the ocean and swim as far as I can." If they stayed here much longer, sunburn might start cooking her.

"Hammond," he said.

"Where's that?" All Erin knew about the area was that they were vaguely close to the Little Creek Joint Expeditionary Base, though her career had never taken her there.

"He's a colonel I served with awhile ago. He lives

in Virginia Beach. And he owes me a favor or three. He'll help us." Gibson spoke with the confidence of a man who wielded favors like blades.

"And does he know about..." She let it trail off, but Gibson knew.

He shook his head. "No. But he's our only hope right now. And there's no reason he needs to know."

Erin wanted to argue, but she wasn't sure if she was doing it reflexively, or if there was something about Hammond that made her hesitate. She didn't know the man, and she didn't want to bring in an outsider, especially when she didn't know what enemies they were facing.

But Gibson was right. They didn't have other options.

Gibson knew his address, and they took off, though they had to duck into a gas station to find a map that could guide them the dozen or so miles to Hammond's place. That took their seven dollars down to five.

This Hammond guy better be home.

But as the sidewalk under their feet ended and they had to walk along the patchy grass that lined the street of an industrial area, doubts began to grow. Erin didn't want to bring any of their mess to a normal person. Her life had been turned upside down and inside out by shifters and magic and all the crap that went along with it.

Colonel Hammond didn't deserve that.

She kept her mouth shut. She couldn't offer another solution, and Gibson knew Hammond. If he vouched for him, the man could handle himself.

She put one foot in front of the other, ignoring the ache from the sandals flapping against her heels. She was tempted to take the shoes off, but there were enough pebbles and broken pieces of glass on the ground that she'd tear her feet to shreds.

The pain from her sandals had a strange settling effect. And every time her gaze strayed over to Gibson and her mind started to wander, there'd be a pinch between her toes and she'd remind herself to stop looking.

Or she'd find him looking right back at her, and her heartbeat threatened to speed up.

It wasn't a difficult walk, but it was monotonous. And every fifteen minutes or so, Gibson made them stop so he could confirm they were headed in the right direction.

Her mouth was dry, and when they passed a local park with an outside water fountain, she made Gibson stop so they could both drink their fill. She didn't suggest that they use the last of their money on a bottle of water, not when they might need it for whatever food they could manage if Hammond wasn't home.

But he was going to be home. She and Gibson were going to make it back to New York. And then they'd kick the asses of every fuckhead who'd tried to hurt their pack.

A nasty smell tickled her nose, and Erin skirted around a mysterious puddle rather than find out what was in it. Another two blocks led them to a busier area with a few pedestrians and shops that were on the shabby end, but had customers in and out.

The sudden roar of an engine had Erin freezing on the corner of one of the streets. A car careened towards her and she raised her hand, as if that might ward it off.

Gibson's strong arms wrapped around her and pulled her back as the car skidded over the curb, right where she'd been standing. The car continued on, bumping back onto the road and speeding off into the distance.

Someone yelled after it, but there was nothing else to do.

Gibson's hold was strong, and it tightened even further. Erin placed her hand over his forearm. She knew she should be breaking his grip, stepping away with a careful thanks and pretending the embrace was nothing more than necessity.

"Are you okay?" Gibson's words ghosted over her ear.

She had to suppress a shiver. Erin managed to nod, but she didn't trust her voice.

His body was hot behind her, a wall of muscle ready to stand between her and the world. She wanted to reach back and wrap an arm around him, even if it would be awkward. She wanted to turn in his embrace and hold on forever.

But she couldn't do that.

With more reluctance than she should have, Erin pulled away. She was vaguely satisfied at the resistance in Gibson's grip. Whatever bound them together, she wasn't alone in the feeling.

*You know exactly what this is.*

Erin ignored that thought.

They walked for at least another hour, maybe two. But no cars tried to mow her down, and she had no excuse to jump into Gibson's arms. Which was for the best.

She had to keep telling herself that.

They ended up on a residential street lined with

houses that had been built back in the seventies, low ranches with big yards.

Gibson knocked on the door, and they both waited with unspoken tension as nearly a minute ticked by. Gibson knocked again.

A muffled sound came from beyond the door, and after a moment it opened to reveal a man in his sixties with patchy gray hair, deep lines around his blue eyes, and pale, sun-reddened skin, who might have been six feet tall before his shoulders started stooping.

"Gibson?" he asked, voice low and full of an officer's command. He might have looked it, but he didn't sound old.

Gibson straightened, and he nodded to the man. "Good afternoon, Colonel. I'm sorry for the short notice, but we need your help."

---

Hammond had gotten old since retiring. It hit Gibson in the chest, that this man who'd been such a vital presence a decade ago had taken on more years than he'd earned. Gibson forced those thoughts aside. Hammond wouldn't appreciate the commentary. And Gibson needed too much help to say a word.

"Colonel," he said, and a part of him snapped right back to three years ago, when life had made sense. "This is my colleague, Erin Jackson. We're..." He wasn't even sure where to start with the explanation.

"Why don't you and your sergeant come inside?" Hammond gestured for them to enter.

It startled Gibson, that he could identify Jackson's rank from nothing but a guess, but the colonel was insightful like that. Or damned creepy, as a lieutenant Gibson used to know once said.

Once inside, he saw Jackson wince as she slid her sandals off. Her feet were blistered and bloody, and Gibson was tempted to sweep her off her feet and carry her to somewhere with a first aid kit to tend to her wounds.

"Bathroom's right there, if you want to get cleaned up," Hammond told her. "Should be some bandages and wound care stuff in the cupboard."

"Thank you, sir."

While Erin went to take care of herself, Hammond led Gibson to the kitchen and offered him water, which Gibson guzzled down gratefully.

"This have something to do with that outfit

you've got going?" Hammond asked. "Private contracting?" he sneered.

"Private security," Gibson corrected. Three years ago, it was his only idea to somehow keep his disparate team of accidental shifters together. Now they were closer than family.

He didn't strain to listen for Jackson. He refused to let himself.

Hammond waited for an explanation. Gibson created one. "I can't go into details, client confidentiality. Jackson and I ended up in town and we were robbed. All we have is the clothes on our back and five dollars between the two of us."

Hammond made an interested sound in the back of his throat. "You didn't call the cops for the theft?"

"Not always the best move in this job," he replied. True, and yet so far from relevant at this moment. "We can be out of your hair in the morning, but we need a place to crash."

"Your people coming to get you?" Of course Hammond would snag on the most obvious source of their problems.

"You hear about that business in Germany a few years back?" Gibson wasn't about to tell him the whole story, but word got around, even to retired officers.

He nodded. "Some weird shit went down."

"And it's still going down, but you don't want to be a part of it. And part of that weird shit means Er—Jackson and I are having issues with phones right now." The colonel's cordless phone was sitting on the counter. Gibson picked it up and pressed the speaker button.

No signal.

He hoped it was enough to keep Hammond from noticing Gibson's slip up.

"Did you break my goddamn phone, soldier?" Hammond scowled, voice rising loud enough to make a drill sergeant blush.

"It will work tomorrow. And if it doesn't, you can Venmo me."

"What the hell is Venmo?" Hammond shook his head and scowled. "Never mind. I'm getting pizza. What kind do you want?"

An hour later, Gibson, Jackson, and Hammond sat around the kitchen table scarfing down enough pepperoni pizza to feed a battalion.

They ate with the kind of single minded focus of the starving, even if Hammond had offered them snacks as soon as they'd settled in. And before Gibson knew it, the pizza was gone and a yawn took him by surprise.

Erin excused herself first, leaving Gibson and Hammond alone again. If the colonel had been thinking of ways to finagle more information from Gibson, he didn't bring it up. Instead, he launched into a story about his time in the Gulf involving a lizard, a bottle of whiskey, and a contortion that Gibson was absolutely certain was impossible.

He was about to share a story of his own when another yawn racked him.

"Sounds like you've had a busy day," said Hammond. "And I'm beat, anyway. We'll talk in the morning."

It was a warning not to sneak off without saying goodbye, and Gibson would heed it. "Good night."

Upstairs, Jackson wasn't in their room.

Their room with only one bed.

Shit.

There was a couch downstairs. Gibson could sneak out, but his feet were lead. Besides, if any magic mojo came their way, he needed to be with Jackson. He wasn't letting her fight her battles alone.

The door open and Jackson slipped in, hair wet and a towel wrapped around her body. Damp tendrils clung to her neck, and a drip of water slid past her collarbone.

He needed to stop its progress with his tongue.

Instead he jerked his gaze away.

Jackson paused before reaching for a folded stack of clothes on the dresser. "Sorry. I forgot to take these with me. Hammond let me borrow some of his daughter's things."

Gibson nodded, not saying a word. She scooped up the clothes and backed out. He had a minute to calm down, to get his body under control and act like the goddamned adult that he was.

He wasn't going to look at the bed.

A few minutes later, Jackson came back wearing a clean set of pajamas. Gibson grabbed his own stack of borrowed clothes—from Hammond, not his daughter—and came back just as quick.

Jackson had a pillow in her hands and tossed it to the ground. "I can take the floor," she offered.

"No way." He didn't care about chivalry or any of that bullshit, but he had some fucking standards. "I can sleep on the floor."

"You're not sleeping on the floor," she countered. "Bed's big enough for both of us, I guess."

His mind flashed to the night before, to their entangled limbs and bruised hearts. Gibson had exactly zero doubts where things would lead if he let himself lie beside Erin Jackson. "I'll take the floor," he repeated.

"That's going to kill your back." Jackson's face was just as stubborn as his.

The need to kiss her was almost overwhelming.

"I'm forty, Jackson, not eighty. I can handle a night on the carpet. Now toss me the damned blanket." He wasn't backing down.

After a second, Jackson rolled her eyes and shoved a blanket at him. Gibson laid down and absolutely did not let out a small groan when his back protested. He was fine. And he wasn't old.

In his active duty days, he could sleep anytime, anywhere. But over the last three years, he'd lost the skill. Eventually he did drift off, but it might have been an hour or more later. He expected pleasant, or possibly frustrating dreams of Erin Gibson.

He jerked awake when he heard her scream.

# CHAPTER EIGHT

Erin couldn't see anything. When she tried to open her eyes, she realized they already were. And that was when the panic set in. She sucked in fast breaths and reached out, trying to figure out where she was and what was going on. She could barely extend her arms before they hit the stone-hard surface that encircled her.

Her limbs were heavy as lead, but she tried to move, to wedge herself against the tight walls and climb up. But before she could get any purchase, the wall around her lost all its firmness and she fell back down, barely scrambling to her feet before it solidified.

"Help!" she screamed, her voice echoing through the empty void. Panic surged as the wall brushed against her fingers, the circumference around her tightening. Erin tried to move, but the wall was pressing against both arms now, and in a few seconds she wouldn't be able to breathe.

"Gibson!" Where was he? Had he already been crushed in a hole like this? "Jericho!" It tore out of the root of her soul as the final crushing weight of the hole closed in.

And then she wasn't in a hole at all. She blinked her eyes open and could see, but it wasn't any better. A masked figure loomed over her, a hand holding a strange, almost familiar device.

The figure sneered at her. "Kneel." It was a woman's voice.

The command punched her in the gut and Erin collapsed to her knees, pain impacting up her thighs and into her hips. There wasn't an ounce of resistance. The woman's word was her deed. Fear burned deep. How could she fight if she couldn't resist?

What was the woman going to do to her?

"Where are you?" the masked figure demanded, her voice cutting over her skin, sharp enough to make her bleed.

Erin choked as she struggled to get the words out, all of them fighting to be spoken at once, following her command. "I'm right here."

The figure reared a hand back, not the one holding the device. But she didn't hit Erin. "Where is your *body*?" She stressed the last word, as if Erin and her body weren't connected.

What was she supposed to say? She was *here*. The woman had control. But it wasn't the right answer and she knew it. Where *was* her body? The knowledge was a kernel deep inside of her, and she could almost speak it, almost reveal the truth.

She had to speak. Her tongue burned. Then something yanked on the back of her neck and shook her by the shoulders. Erin's eyes flew open again, chest heaving as she came back to her body, to herself.

A nightmare. Just a dream.

A dark figure hovered over her, and panic threatened to surge once more before she heard the voice that could always call her home.

"Erin, wake up. You're dreaming." His voice had a strange battlefield calm, like he could strike down any enemy without a doubt. His hands were on either side of her head, boxing her in. But she didn't feel trapped. Gibson wasn't trapping her, he was protecting her from the rest of the world.

"Jericho," she whispered, knowing her trembling

voice gave away too much, but too shaken to care. "It felt so real."

His eyes raked over her face, worry etched in the lines on his forehead. "You were screaming. It sounded..." He hesitated, and after a second let the sentence hang.

Erin knew she should say something, should reassure him she was fine and that they could both go back to sleep as if nothing had happened. But she feared that if he moved even an inch further away from her, she'd start shaking and never stop.

"I've got you," Gibson whispered, pulling her close and shifting his body so he was pressed tight against her. He wrapped his arms around her tightly, anchoring her in the present moment. His solid presence grounded her in reality, and she focused on the steady rhythm of his heartbeat against her ear.

With Gibson her shield, the memory of the nightmare began to fade. Sleep, though? Yeah, that wasn't happening any time soon. The thought of closing her eyes and jumping back into that hole or facing that... monster... made her stomach roil.

And she didn't want to be alone.

She snuggled closer into Gibson's chest, her emotions raw and right on the surface. Her fear went a bit gauzy, a thing she could ignore and bat away like it was nothing. Gibson was supposed to be off limits. Erin knew she shouldn't cling to him, but she couldn't make her fingers uncurl from where they were wrapped in the fabric of his shirt.

He let her hold on until her breathing lost its jitteriness and her heartbeat evened out. Erin couldn't ask for more. She knew that. Knew she had to let him get back to sleep. They had a lot to face in the morning, and one of them needed to be fully conscious.

But when Gibson made a move to roll away, Erin tightened her grip. Their eyes met, gazes locked for a frozen second. And between one heartbeat and the next, the moment changed from one of comfort to something completely different.

Something heated and needy.

Erin didn't move fast. The urgency that had driven them at the motel was gone. Tonight it felt different. The room was dark around them, the moonlight flickering in through the window promising to keep their secrets.

She gave Gibson plenty of time to pull back. Instead his lips met hers, the kiss their secret shared in the darkness.

She wrapped her arms around his neck and

opened her mouth as his tongue tangled with hers. Fear, need, longing, it was all there and poured into the kiss like a desperate magic potion she hoped could give her the one thing she wasn't supposed to have.

His tongue weaved its spell on her, the intensity strong enough to make her shiver. And then there was the feeling of his cock hardening against her, the reminder of exactly what he could do to her, making her own body heat and crave all he could give her.

Erin's gasp seemed to ignite something within Gibson, and he groaned into the kiss, pressing her against the bed until she was trapped by sensation. His touch was sure and eager, his hand running down her side until he found the hem of her shirt, but he didn't pull it up. They stayed in that kiss for what seemed like forever, lost in the moment, in the intensity of the thing they both refused to name.

Erin finally had to come up for air, gasping as if she'd forgotten how to breathe. The raw need that tore through her reflected in his eyes, the promise that tonight was a moment out of time, just for them. It made her smile and made her a bit brave, as if she was suddenly sure that there was no request she could make tonight that Gibson wouldn't grant her.

She reached for the hem of his shirt and pulled it over his head, letting her hands roam over his hard chest while their lips crashed back together. The dark hair that covered his chest was peppered with more gray than the hair on his head, but all it did was remind Erin that Gibson had lived his life, and that life had brought him here.

To her.

"Erin," he whispered against her lips. She'd give just about anything for him to keep calling her that, to say it *that* way, like she was precious.

Like she was his.

While she was lost in the kiss, he managed to finagle her shirt mostly off, and she helped him get it the rest of the way. Gibson pulled back and stared down at her, and his eyes seemed to glow in the moonlight. It had to be a trick, but Erin didn't care. Not when he bent down and took one of her nipples into his mouth, licking and sucking until she squirmed. His tongue traced patterns around her nipple, teeth teasing only enough to make her arch up against him.

It was torture, but the kind that made her beg for more.

"Please." She couldn't stop the plea, her voice barely a whisper. "Jericho." The heat between them was an inferno, one that had to blaze out on its own. Nothing could stop them now, not with the way her body ached for his. Not with the way his rigid cock brushed against her, teasing her.

Gibson's lips slid down her body, leaving a trail of wet kisses and lingering heat. Erin's breath hitched in anticipation, her heart pounding in her ears. She needed everything he wanted to give her and couldn't help but spread her legs further apart in invitation.

When Gibson finally reached her slick folds, his warm breath fanned across her sensitive flesh, making her shiver with need. Without hesitation, his mouth closed over her, sucking gently as his tongue flicked back and forth. Erin let out a deep moan, her fingers curling into the already wrinkled sheets beneath her, unable to control the overwhelming sensations coursing through her.

"Jericho," she gasped, her voice laden with desire. He responded by sliding two fingers inside her wet heat, slowly pumping them in and out while his tongue continued its relentless assault on her swollen sex. God, the man knew what he was doing. It brought her to the edge, her body tensing as she held onto the precipice of a cresting wave of need.

"Please... more," Erin gasped, her hips bucking against Gibson's face. He only increased the intensity of his actions, driving her over the edge with a throaty groan. Her orgasm crashed over her, her entire body shaking as she rode it out.

As the tremors subsided, Erin looked down at Gibson, his eyes bright with need of his own. He crawled back up her body, capturing her lips in a heated kiss she couldn't deny. The primal intimacy of the act sent another jolt of pleasure through her, and she wrapped her hand around his throbbing cock.

His masculine groan was its own reward as she stroked him firmly. Gibson's eyes squeezed shut, his head thrown back as he gave himself over to sensation. She felt powerful with him like this, at her mercy and begging without words for more.

"I've got you." She stroked faster, her grip just enough to push him over the edge. With a deep, guttural groan, Gibson's body tensed as he found his release, his seed spilling over her hand and onto her stomach.

Erin smiled, more than a little smug, as she felt Gibson relax into the mattress beneath them, their bodies still intertwined. He blinked his eyes open slowly, as if coming back to himself, and gazed up at her with an expression she couldn't quite decipher. It made her breath catch.

She leaned in close to kiss him tenderly, afraid that if she didn't, one of them might speak. And with her body still singing with sensation, she couldn't let that happen.

She turned so she was lying on her stomach and hummed contentedly as Jericho traced his fingers down her spine, making some sort of pattern that only he could see. She could fall asleep like this and forget all her troubles, especially the nightmare.

"When did you get this tattoo?" he asked, lips fluttering over it.

"What?" She propped herself on her elbow and contorted, trying to see her back. "I don't have a tattoo."

Afterglow evaporating in a heartbeat, Erin jumped off the bed and sprinted across the hall to the bathroom, uncaring she was naked. Jericho followed right after her.

She flipped on the light switch and squinted against the sudden brightness. A harried search through the drawers turned up a handheld mirror and she turned her back to the main mirror, checking out her reflection.

Right on her left shoulder blade was a swirl of black ink that might have been a tribal tattoo, but that had never been Erin's style.

"They did this to me." She was trying not to panic and trying even harder not to yell. She didn't need to summon Hammond. They were asking him too much already. "Those magic bastards. Get it off."

Gibson was at her back. "How? It's a tattoo."

"I don't care if you have to cut the damned thing off, I'm not leaving this bathroom until it's gone."

# CHAPTER NINE

ERIN'S SHOULDER shuddered under Gibson's fingers. Or possibly his own hand was shaking. The dark mark over her scapula seemed to grow more sinister the more he looked at it, the strangely uneven lines emanating some sort of evil he couldn't quite comprehend.

"Get this thing off me, Gibson. Do it now." An edge of panic tinged her voice. This was Erin Fucking Jackson. She could stare down any enemy without giving anything away. And yet she trembled.

"We'll get it off," he promised, mind scrambling. "Maybe we can have Hammond call Vi, she'll know something." He didn't want to bring the colonel any deeper into this than necessary, but he'd do it if it meant keeping Jackson safe.

"I want it gone now." Her voice got eerily calm. "Cut if off if you have to, I don't care."

"I do." His hand flexed on her shoulder, unable to break away. "I'm not cutting this off you, not before we explore our options." He tried to put the weight of command into his voice; instead he knew he sounded like the concerned lover he was. He couldn't bear to see his mate in pain.

"It's not your fucking body," Erin bit out, her eyes narrowed and staring at him through the mirror. "I can take it. And who knows what magic bullshit this thing is doing to me, to us. I bet this is why we can't use phones, why your stuff disappeared. Or do you have another explanation for a magically appearing shitty tattoo?"

He thought it looked kind of stylish, except for the evil magic. But now was not the time for Gibson's sartorial opinions. "I know you can take it, you can take anything. But leaving you bleeding and screaming is only going to make things worse." He clung to that logic. If Jackson couldn't slow down, maybe he had to come at it another way.

She paused. Breathed. Then took another deep

breath. "Fine, if you want to try something first, try it. But when that doesn't work, get a knife, a candle, I don't care. Whatever it takes, Gibson. We need to get rid of this thing tonight."

"Okay," he said, though he still refused to do anything that would hurt her. He just needed to figure out how to remove a magical tattoo from the woman he... from his packmate without hurting her, only using what he could find in the colonel's bathroom cabinets.

Easy.

Or it would be, if he had any reason to think fluffy white towels might do something to a magical tattoo. Every second he hesitated, Jackson became more tense. Gibson was going to demand remedial magic lessons as soon as they got home. Maybe he'd never cast a spell, but he'd like to know strategies to counteract them.

"Didn't you say something about salt?" he asked.

"I thought maybe the sea water interrupted the spell or whatever. What do you think? Tape a bandage full of rock salt over the thing and hope that does it?" She spun around and gave him a challenging look.

Gibson wasn't about to admit that her idea was even better than what he'd been imagining.

Her breath caught, and he realized she was staring at his lips. Gibson stood close to her, practically trapping her against the counter. It would take less than a single step for him to close the distance between them and let their bodies brush together.

He shouldn't. He knew that in a distant part of his mind.

But he still leaned forward.

Their lips touched and electricity surged through his veins. Erin's arms wrapped around his neck, yanking him closer as the intensity of the kiss grew. Their emotions poured into each other—fear, desperation, and a longing that they both knew they had to ignore.

And yet...

Gibson splayed his hand high on her back, covering the mark as if that alone would be enough to banish it. He drew her against him as their tongues danced, savoring the taste and feel of one another. He couldn't help but let out a growl of approval as Erin arched against him, his body firing back to life.

He wanted to take her right there, to hitch her

hips up onto the counter and slide into her until she screamed in ecstasy. The draw between them was too real, too strong, to fight for long.

But he had to.

Gibson tore himself away and they both gasped for air. He couldn't stop staring at Erin's flushed face and swollen lips. He wanted more of her, every last inch, but if bits and scraps were all he ever got, he'd hold the memories close.

There would never be another Erin Jackson for him. She was it.

The enormity of the realization pressed down on him, and the words got lost in his throat. He wanted to confess... something. Devotion? Love? It was all too big, and no word felt quite right.

But all that was swept away when he moved his hand and saw the mark on her shoulder in the mirror once more.

The *smudged* mark on her shoulder.

Without warning, Gibson jerked Jackson around so he could look at her back. And there he noticed it, a thumbprint right along the edge of where the mark had been, smudged like marker.

Gibson licked his thumb and pressed it against the mark, rubbing at it. His thumb came away dark with ink. "Look." He held up his thumb for her to see. "It's coming off."

"Really?" Jackson's face scrunched up. "Did you just lick your thumb? What the hell?"

"That's what you're worried about?" He could have said something about licking her all over, but even with the taste of her kiss still on his tongue, he held himself back. He placed his thumb back over the mark and tried to get more off.

"Stop!" Jackson jerked her shoulder forward. "Don't get the magic ink on your skin. Find some nail polish remover or something. Or makeup remover. Hell, just get a wash cloth and soap."

Both nail polish remover and makeup remover were unlikely to be in the retired colonel's guest bathroom, but they both tore through the cabinets. And Gibson was the one that got lucky, snagging a small bottle that stood next to a vial of blue nail polish, a reminder of the colonel's adult daughter.

He couldn't find cotton balls, so he poured the liquid on a wash cloth and started to rub gently against Jackson's skin, careful not to abrade it.

"Harder," she demanded in a way that made his cock jerk.

Their eyes met in the mirror, heat flaring for just a second before they both cracked into grins.

"I'll show you hard." He pressed the cloth harder until she had to press back against him to keep from bending over.

It took time. After a few minutes, Gibson had to rinse the cloth and apply more remover. And still he could see the faint outline of the mark. He didn't know if the magic was good to the last drop, and he wasn't going to risk it.

He hoped removing it was enough.

Jackson's skin was red and threatening to bleed in a few places by the time he switched from nail polish remover to soap. But nearly an hour after he'd started, he was satisfied that the mark was gone, her shoulder bare and as devoid of magic as they could make it.

"Do you think that will do it?" she asked, hand snaking over her shoulder and fingers flirting with the edge of where the mark had been.

Gibson let his hand cover hers and told himself he was comforting her as a packmate, the same way he would anyone else. "Yes." He didn't let himself doubt. There was no point to it.

She leaned back into him and he let himself enjoy the sensation. But he didn't let himself gather her in his arms and hold tight. They'd crossed so many lines, he had to start backtracking. He had to fix this thing between them.

But when they went back to the guest room, he crawled into bed beside her. And when she curled against him, he wrapped an arm around her.

Boundaries could wait until morning.

# CHAPTER TEN

Gibson wasn't much of a cook. Sure, he could make rations well enough to survive, but he'd never be a chef. But the least he could do was fix breakfast for Hammond. Using Hammond's ingredients, of course, but bacon and eggs was easy enough. And the longer he stared at the bacon, the less he had to think about the retired colonel staring at him, eyebrows raised in question.

Gibson poked at the eggs. He was a grown man. He could have one damned conversation. But he really wished that Jackson wasn't in the shower right now. He could use a bit of a buffer between himself and the colonel's prying eyes.

"That's one hell of a soldier you got there," Hammond said lightly.

Gibson's grip tightened on the spatula, but he didn't let himself react. "She is," he agreed.

He knew where this was going. Where it had to go. After decades in the military, Hammond would always be more soldier than civilian, more officer than man. And if Gibson thought that *he* took chain of command seriously, Hammond put him to shame.

"Did the two of you serve together?" Hammond asked. Gibson turned to fiddle with the coffee maker, as if that might soften the blow of the implication in his words.

"We were in Germany at the same time, but different units." He hadn't met Erin Jackson until after the kidnapping.

Gibson had no idea how he would have felt if they'd met before, if the thing between them would have flared to life when it truly was against the rules and not just something they shouldn't do.

Hammond made a strange noise, and it caught Gibson's attention.

"What?" he asked.

Hammond turned towards his fridge. "I've got a bunch of flavored creamer. You want hazelnut?" he asked, grabbing the container and shaking it.

Okay. So they weren't talking about Germany or

whatever it was that had made Hammond change the subject with all the finesse of a weightlifter trying to break a world record.

"Jackson works for me," Gibson said firmly. It was the truth. She worked for him. And she was his... He couldn't let the word out.

If the last two days had taught him anything, it was that his feelings for her were real. They were something that couldn't be ignored. But they had to be put aside, at least until they were home safe.

"So, were you all just having a conference call last night?" Hammond asked, his grin turning sly.

A growl threatened to bubble up out of the back of Gibson's throat. Last night. Joy. Terror. Pleasure. It all swirled around in his head. Hammond had most likely heard them while they were in the bathroom, but there was nothing sexy there except for the one kiss. Gibson refused to rise to the bait.

"I know what I'm doing," he said.

"Let's hope so." Hammond's tone made it clear that he was finished with the conversation. But then the colonel shifted and stared at Gibson with his arms crossed. "I get it. Sneaking around, the excitement of possibly getting caught. A woman who's strong enough to talk back. But sometimes, you think with your dick, and you end up divorced three times, sitting on your back porch doing Sudoku puzzles and reminiscing about the good old days."

There was a lot that Gibson could say to that. He could have argued that his heart wasn't the issue, and that his mind, body, and dick were all in alignment. He could have told Hammond that Erin Jackson was the only woman on the entire planet for him, and that he'd known it for a long time. But Hammond was an old army buddy, not the kind of guy Gibson had heart-to-heart conversations with.

"That's not the problem," Gibson replied.

"It never is," Hammond said, with the confidence of someone who had no idea how deeply he was treading in the waters of their conversation. He couldn't sense the undercurrents, nor could he understand the context. Gibson had no intention of explaining it to him.

Hammond opened his mouth to speak again, but Gibson glared at him. The old colonel laughed.

"Don't worry, it's not about you and the young lady," he assured Gibson. "Well, maybe a little. But not about sex."

If it was just about sex, Gibson's life would be much simpler.

"I've got this old rust heap of a car," Hammond said. "It's been gathering dust in my garage for a couple of years now. I keep tinkering with it, but you know how it is."

Gibson didn't, but he said nothing.

"I want you and Jackson to take it. I think it'll get you up to New York. And this." Hammond opened the drawer under the coffee maker and handed a thick envelope to Gibson.

"I can't take this," Gibson protested. He didn't count the bills, but there had to be over a thousand dollars inside. "Really, you've helped us enough."

"How else are you planning to get home? With no money, no phone, and no car?" Hammond challenged. "I don't need the car. Frankly, you'd be doing me a favor. And as for the money, come and visit me sometime and let me win it back off you in a game of poker. How does that sound?"

They needed the money too much for Gibson to refuse it again. And he could always pay Hammond back, either in a card game or by sending a check. Gibson pocketed the money.

"There's a chance the car won't make it back in one piece," Gibson warned, though he didn't want to go into detail about what might happen. How did a person even begin to explain magical damage to an insurance adjuster?

Hammond shrugged. "As I said, it's a junk heap.

It should run. But if I don't get it back, I don't get it back. And my daughter will be happy to park in the garage the next time she visits."

"Thank you," Gibson said, sincerely grateful.

———

Erin's skin was clean, and her hair was still a little damp, but she had managed to find a hair tie and pull it back. The clothes borrowed from Hammond's daughter were a bit big and hung off of her, but they were clean. Everything about this day was looking up, even if her shoulder was still a little raw from rubbing it so roughly last night to get the mark off.

But the mark was gone, and that probably meant that she and Gibson were no longer being chased by evil witches. She had given her body a complete look over in the shower, with judicious use of her hand mirror.

A woman was not meant to see herself from so many angles, but Erin didn't spot any other suspicious tattoos, and she was satisfied that she was safe, for now. At least safe from witches.

Her heart, on the other hand?

She heard Gibson and Hammond talking in the kitchen, but it was the smell of bacon that truly summoned her. Gibson stood beside the stove, a spatula in one hand, and poked at the frying meat. He served her a plate which she took gratefully, trying not to enjoy the way Jericho Gibson looked in the kitchen. She'd never seen him cook before. It was almost disconcertingly domestic.

"Hammond has a car for us," Gibson said. "One day of driving, and we should be home."

That was good. That was great, even. She was just going to ignore the tiny bit of her that was disappointed that her alone time with Gibson was coming to an end.

Erin dug into her breakfast, focusing more on her food than the conversation that Gibson and Hammond were engaged in. Clearly, they had been talking for some time, but at this point, she couldn't care. She didn't say anything. She was too grateful for the night of reprieve. Hammond had stepped up where a lot of people wouldn't. He hadn't asked questions. If he wanted to gossip or talk about her behind her back, there wasn't much she could do about that. And she wasn't sure she cared.

"You said you two served in Germany together?" Hammond asked.

"Not together," Gibson said, in a way that

sounded like he was repeating it. "Yes, we were both in Germany. About three years ago."

Hammond set his coffee cup down a little harder than necessary, and it made Erin look up. Now Hammond was looking at them, an unreadable look in his eyes. But this time, it wasn't gossipy. "I heard about something going down there. Didn't like the way that played out. You had a career ahead of you." He said it to Gibson, but it was true of Erin too. She hadn't been ready to retire when she was forced out. Her contract wasn't even up. But the US military had a way of making internal problems go away.

"What did you hear about that?" Gibson asked.

Erin wanted to know too. There'd been lawyers and threats. Heavy implications that if they talked, their easy retirements would disappear, and the paperwork could change, even if that wasn't exactly legal. What was Erin supposed to say? That she'd been kidnapped? That some strange evil wizard had turned her into a werewolf? She didn't have anyone to talk to. And it wasn't like she could tell her family. But clearly, the story had gotten around. At least parts of it.

"Just heard about some funny business," Hammond said with a shrug.

"Maybe don't share it around," Gibson warned.

"We all know some things are better left in the past."

Silence hung between them for a long moment before Hammond nodded. "How about I show you the car?" he offered.

"Sure," Gibson agreed.

Erin finished her meal quickly and grabbed the rest of the dishes, adding hers to the dishwasher alongside Gibson's and Hammond's. She stared at the cordless phone on the countertop for several seconds before she mustered up the courage to give it a try.

There was a dial tone. She let out a sob of joy and was glad that no one was there to hear it. The mark was gone. She was right. Things were looking up.

She quickly dialed the first phone number she could think of: Owen's. The phone rang and rang, but there was no answer. The goddamned bastard didn't pick up. She was going to give him so much shit for this as soon as she got home.

There was so much to say that putting it into a single message was difficult, but she managed. She told Owen that she was safe, Gibson was with her, and that they were making their way by car from Virginia to New York. Then she hung up. She would let Hammond know that Owen might call him back.

Hopefully, the colonel wouldn't mind acting as an answering service for the day.

In the harsh light of the morning, Erin saw Gibson and Hammond standing beside a station wagon that looked like it had barely survived the war—possibly the Revolutionary War. Rust covered the wheel rims, one of the back windows stubbornly remained slightly open, and a glance through the windows showed cloth seats that looked like a wolf had gnawed on them. Erin's doubt was evident on her face.

Hammond chuckled. "She starts," he promised. "I just tested it last week."

It wasn't like Erin had room to argue. And the car was better than walking. Gibson's hand hovered over the roof, as if he were going to pet it, but thought better when he realized just how much of it was made of rust. He lowered his hand gently. "Let's get going."

"Let's."

# CHAPTER ELEVEN

THE CRACKED leather of the steering wheel bit into Gibson's hands as he drove down the old highway, the towering trees encroaching ever closer to the car. Beside him, Jackson lay her head against the window and watched the scenery fly by as if this was some kind of vacation road trip.

The engine wheezed and sputtered whenever they had to shift gears, but it had been miles and miles since they'd last seen a traffic light. If he didn't look too closely at the car interior—or breathe too deeply of the embedded smell of cigarette smoke and age—it was almost pleasant.

"Any updates on our route?" Gibson asked, his voice a bit scratchy from disuse and thirst. He reached for a water bottle in the center console before he remembered they'd finished the drinks from their brief lunch awhile ago and thrown them out at the last gas station.

Jackson shifted in her seat to trace her finger over the old paper map in her lap. "We're on track. More than half way there since we're out of Baltimore. I think we'll be in Pennsylvania soon."

"Soon as in ten miles or soon as in three hours?" He hadn't quite realized just how long their trip would be without the use of freeways. But they wanted to avoid the trouble that came with a lot of people on the road, in case the witches caught up with them.

"I guess we'll see." A small smile teased her lips.

Gibson wanted to reach out and take her hand. If he were driving with his mate, he would. He *was* driving with his mate, but he couldn't. They'd had a day's worth of road for him to say something about their nights together, yet he hadn't uttered a word.

He told himself it was because they were stuck together in the car. If—when—they had this conversation, it needed to be somewhere they could both walk away from, not a stuffy station wagon that was as old as he was.

The sun was low in the sky, casting long shadows as Gibson pulled into a gas station. The tank wasn't empty, but they could both stretch their legs and take a minute to themselves.

Jackson popped her door open and stood beside the pump, stretching her hands high and leaning from side to side, letting out a deep sound of satisfaction that Gibson did his best to ignore.

The twitch of his cock told him just how poorly that was going.

She shot him a smile. "I'm going to head inside. Do you want a snack or something?"

"Just something to drink, we'll stop for dinner in an hour or two," he replied. She gave him a quick nod and jogged towards the store. Gibson watched her until she disappeared inside, the longing to walk beside her almost strong enough to make him chase after her.

Instead, Gibson took a deep breath and inhaled the crisp air tinged with the scent of gasoline. The station was between two small towns in Maryland, and there was a decent amount of traffic passing on the old state highway.

The gas station butted up against dense woods, and Gibson's wolf pulled at him to run towards them, strong enough that he actually took a step and nearly tripped over the gas hose.

He shook his head and forced himself to look away. He looked for Jackson beyond the windows of the gas station, but with all the advertisements plastered on the glass, he couldn't make her out.

It was fine. They could part for a handful of minutes. She could take care of herself.

He kept expecting something bad to happen. It still wasn't quite real in his mind that he'd gotten Jackson back and she was safe, that he could reach out and touch her. Or, well, he could when she was back from her quest to find snacks.

The gas pump clicked off, signaling that the tank was full. Gibson quickly replaced the nozzle and screwed the cap back onto the car, and sent up a quick prayer that there weren't any leaks in the gas tank. The car had held up well enough so far, and it was roughly the size of a tank, so Gibson wasn't concerned about its battle readiness. But he still half-expected the engine to sputter out at the worst time possible and for a coven of witches to descend in attack.

Wind gusted around him, battering his hair into his eyes. He slicked it back and glared at the sky, as if that might do anything.

Where was Jackson?

He looked down at his wrist only to realize he wasn't wearing a watch. She'd been gone for several minutes. She should be back by now. Or possibly he was going crazy. They weren't in a rush. She didn't have to hurry through her snack choosing process in the hopes that they made it back home before midnight.

Something was wrong.

His instincts screamed it at him, tendrils digging deep and trying to pull him away from the car. This time there was no fuel hose to trip him up, and he was stepping past the pumps, at the edge of the woods before he realized it.

As Gibson stood there, the distant echo of a strange noise tickled his ears, and he had to strain to hear more. What was it? A howl? A roar?

No. It was a scream, one pulled from the deepest darkness of someone's soul and yanking deep inside of Gibson, a hook around the part of him that was called to help.

He took off running towards the woods, unable to look back towards the gas station or pause to think things through. A distant part of him knew this was wrong, knew he shouldn't be wandering alone in the forest, even if he was part forest creature.

The sound cut off and Gibson froze.

It was darker in the woods, the setting sun no longer quite reaching to the dark shadows under the trees. Wind whistled through the branches, but there were no chirping birds, no prancing wildlife.

It was as if darkness was chewing the place up from the inside.

And someone had screamed.

He moved slower now, taking his time and choosing his steps carefully. After a minute or two, Gibson looked back, but he couldn't see the gas station, as if the woods had somehow managed to cut him off from the rest of the world.

A fanciful thought.

Or would be. If he hadn't landed smack dab in the middle of a maelstrom of magical bullshit.

He had to turn back. The scream had gone quiet, and he saw no signs of life. The smart move now would be to go to the gas station and call the cops. They could comb the woods for trouble, and they'd do it better than him.

"H—help..." It was a whispering cry that floated past him, somehow coming from every direction at once.

Gibson strained to hear more, to figure out which way to step. He couldn't turn away if someone was hurt right there.

He should have brought Jackson with him, he could use the backup. He shook his head, it didn't matter now.

"Hel..." There was that sound again. This time Gibson could pinpoint it coming from behind a tree just a little bit off the path. He stepped towards it.

And darkness barreled into him. A shadow fought him, impossible claws made of darkness and smoke swiping at him and ripping a hole in his shirt, missing his skin by only a whisper.

He stumbled back, eyes wide with shock and stuttering confusion. What the hell was going on? Deep in his mind he knew about something like this, a beast made of shadows that could only be fought with light. His packmate, Andre, had fought one before.

But where was Gibson going to find light in the encroaching darkness?

The ball of dark came at him again, and even knowing it should be impossible, Gibson struck back. And hit something. It wasn't darkness, and it didn't feel like flesh. Instead, his hand scraped against a bundle of sticks and leaves, as if the shadow was a cloak around a tree-creature.

He didn't have time to study it. No matter how hard he hit, the creature fought back, and Gibson was in unfamiliar terrain and in the wrong form. If he was in his wolf skin, this would be nothing. But fighting unarmed as a man was a reminder of how weak he could be.

He took another step back and stumbled over an unseen log, going to one knee and wincing as the shock of it reverberated up his leg.

The forest monster loomed, stalking close, an unholy light glimmering impossibly from the darkness at its core.

A howl tore through the air around him, a hundred times more real than the sound that had lured him, and Erin Jackson pounced on the creature, her teeth digging in and shaking until it was nothing but a pile of sticks flying through the air as the force of her fury dislodged them.

Gibson struggled to his feet. The pain in his leg was no good, a promise that walking would be no treat, but he wouldn't let Jackson face the beast alone.

She bared her teeth at the remnants of the twig-monster, and Gibson half expected it to begin to reform. They both waited, breaths heavy and dread a blanket over both of them. But nothing else attacked.

But Gibson didn't let his guard down, not even when he let himself run a hand through Jackson's glossy fur.

The magic had found them once more.

# CHAPTER TWELVE

GIBSON'S WEIGHT was heavy on Erin's shoulders as they stumbled back to the car. Luckily she'd been able to remove her clothes before shifting forms, otherwise she'd be stumbling naked through the woods, and that was not fun in human form.

He groaned and leaned harder against her, and that made Erin worry more than anything. Gibson was a tough old wolf. She'd seen him walk off a stab wound once. Whatever that magical monster had done, it couldn't be good.

What if he...

No. She refused to think it.

She got them back to the station wagon and had never been more happy to see a junk heap. Gibson shifted his weight and walked on his own power towards the driver side door.

"I'm driving," she said before his hand hit the handle.

"I can drive." He sounded more angry than pained, a hint of gruffness and growl that really would have done it for her in other circumstances.

Okay, she was kidding herself. It still did it for her. But she was sitting on her own well of anger and the more she noticed the pale tint of Gibson's skin and the tight lines around his mouth, the angrier she got.

He could have died. He'd walked into that forest alone, knowing there was evil magic after them, and he hadn't called to her for backup.

What the actual hell.

She was tempted to say something about it. To ask if he thought she was suddenly incompetent because she'd had his dick in her mouth. But Erin kept her mouth shut. That wasn't the problem between them, and to mention it would only hurt Gibson.

"Let me drive, Jericho." His name hung between them, the promise of everything they could be, if they could find a way past their own hesitations.

He shuffled to the other side and slid into the

passenger seat. The backseat was bigger, spacious enough that he could lounge, and she almost suggested that. But he could walk on his own, and that meant he was well enough to decide where he would sit.

She picked up the bag of snacks she'd dropped outside the car once she'd realized that Gibson was gone, some undeniable pull demanding she follow him into the woods.

"They had a display case for burner phones," she said as she clipped her seatbelt, grasping for normalcy. "Unfortunately they were sold out."

"We'll be home soon enough." Gibson took a deep breath before reaching over his shoulder to grab his seat belt and fasten it.

Erin said nothing, instead putting the car into gear and pulling onto the road. She could pretend everything was okay for a few minutes. Her worry for Gibson didn't lessen.

A sudden pothole had Gibson cursing and curling his hand over the window ledge, as if that might give him some leverage.

Heart in her chest, Erin pulled the car down a small drive marked Historic Route and parked in an unlit parking lot that was probably for a historical marker she couldn't see.

"It's fine," Gibson protested.

She came round to his side of the car and unclipped his belt when he wouldn't. His masculine scent mixed with the woodsy smell all around them did a number on her, but she refused to react.

"Come on, stand up," she said, trying to sound professional, like she'd be this worried for anyone else. "Let me check you out. Hopefully that monster didn't manage to brand you like they did me." She shivered at the thought, concern transforming from worry simply about injury to something even more dire.

Gibson stood, expression clear that he was humoring her. "I'm fine," he promised. He twisted from side to side, showing his range of motion. "Want me to do jumping jacks?"

Yes. Maybe. Not that she'd say that out loud.

"Lift your arms again," she said instead, mentally cataloging the body parts he'd been favoring.

Gibson complied, wincing only slightly as he raised his arm above his head.

"Twist," she instructed, gaze heavy on him.

"I already did that," he protested.

"For me." And if there was a bit of something

else, something they definitely weren't talking about in her voice, well, Gibson didn't say anything.

As he twisted, his shirt rode up, and Erin couldn't help but reach up and run her fingers over the exposed skin. Gibson stopped moving, but Erin couldn't pull her hand away.

She let her fingers trace under his shirt and up over his muscles, his skin hot and alive under her hand.

"Erin," Gibson whispered, his voice rough with need. One of them was supposed to be strong, was supposed to resist.

The both kept failing.

Erin surged up and captured his lips with hers. It was a hungry kiss, urgent, their mouths melded together, desperate to make up for all the time they'd wasted ignoring this passionate attraction. Erin's hands roamed over Gibson's chest, feeling the powerful muscles tense beneath her touch as his hands tangled in her hair, holding her close.

Erin's heart raced, blood pumping hard and fast under her skin, a wild rhythm that matched the throb of her desire, and she could feel Gibson's racing just as fast beneath her touch.

They stumbled back, a quick fumble at the back door of the car all it took before they were splayed across the back seat, lips locked together with Erin on top of Jericho, his body a solid bed.

Jericho's fingers were everywhere, in her hair, on her lower back, against her side, up under her shirt. Erin squirmed under him, and ran her hands down his side, feeling every inch of his back and shoulders, his arms, his chest. Skin on skin, mouth on mouth, hands moving everywhere, she needed to get closer.

Jericho's hands were at her waist, but Erin placed her own fingers over his, stilling him. There was something more she wanted, something she needed, even in the tight confines of the car.

She slid down, her finger flicking open the button of his jeans and tugging his zipper before pulling his boxers down slightly.

God, his cock was a beautiful thing, long and hard, the tip crowned with a glossy wetness that spoke of his arousal. The veins coursed along its length, and the skin felt smooth and silky when she ran her fingers along it. She knew exactly what she wanted and took it, sucking him, her lips around his shaft, her tongue working in time with her movements.

Jericho groaned, his body arching into her as he pressed deeper into her mouth. Erin released him just long enough to take a breath before going back for more, licking and teasing his sensitive head. His hips jerked up in response to each movement, pressing his already hard cock even further into her mouth until there was nothing left but pleasure pulsing through them both. He tensed, his hands going to her hair and tugging lightly. He was close, and they both needed more.

But Jericho pulled away, leaving her at his feet, lips swollen and body burning.

"Take your pants off and get up here," he demanded, the words almost too rough to understand.

———

This wasn't Gibson's first time in the back seat of an old station wagon, but it blew every memory so far out of the water that the only thing that existed for him was Erin.

Nothing new really.

And with his cock leaking and demanding more, it would be so easy to pull her on top of him and surge up into her tight heat until nothing separated them.

But he needed a taste.

Erin's eyes widened with excitement as he

issued his command, and Gibson savored the moment. He watched in anticipation as she pushed her pants and panties down, exposing herself to his hungry gaze. His own cock twitched in response and a low growl came from him. He held himself back, pressing his hands against the car door and trying to remain calm.

Then, Erin was on top of him, her eyes burning with desire. Her hands moved to the back of his head, pushing slightly, letting him know what she wanted, what they both needed.

He feasted.

Gibson's hands moved to her hips, then pulled her down onto his mouth, his tongue pressing against her sex, her taste exploding against him.

This was Gibson's true purpose, licking and sucking Erin until she was moaning above him, her body writhing and pressing in against him, trying to get every bit of pleasure she could. His own desire was boiling over, but he contained it, wanting to give her everything before he took anything for himself.

She gasped as his tongue circled around her clit, and he moaned into her as the sound passed through him. His fingers dug into her hips as he continued to worship her body with his own, teasing out every sensation until she was trembling with blissful pleasure.

He could feel the tension in her grow and knew that any moment now, she would crash over the edge into ecstasy.

Gibson shifted his position slightly and thrust two fingers deeply into her core. This sent Erin over the edge and she screamed out his name.

Still, it wasn't enough. He needed the feel of her tight heat wrapped around him, needed her to understand that no one else could ever compare to this. His thumb found her clit and rubbed as she moaned against him.

He had to pull away, just enough to give her a second to breathe, no matter how much he wanted to keep touching. Her eyes were closed, and she was trying to catch her breath.

But they weren't done, far from it.

"Erin," he said, his voice hoarse and deep. He savored the syllables, the way she was his in this moment, that he was hers in ways he couldn't quite fathom and refused to give up.

She opened her eyes and met his gaze.

"I need to fuck you." He wasn't begging, not yet, but his hand was wrapped around his cock and he ached for her.

"God, yes." She crawled on top of him and captured his lips with her own.

Then her hips were right there and he guided his cock to her entrance, groaning as he slid into her.

He closed his eyes, savoring the moment, savoring the feeling of finally being home. Of having her once more. She fit perfectly against him and Gibson didn't know how he could ever give this up, not after he finally knew her taste, her feel. Not after the way she'd written her name on his soul.

She rode him, their bodies hungry for each other. And before long, Erin was gasping again, body rippling around him as she came, orgasm tearing through her.

Gibson was powerless to do anything but follow after, body surging into her and emptying.

He could have died happy there, with Erin in his arms in their little slice of highway far away from anyone else. He held onto her, not willing to let go even as he knew they had to continue on their journey.

It was a slow thing, getting their clothes back on, cleaning their bodies as best they could. Gibson couldn't make himself crawl out of the backseat, as if that would be the final confession, the last moment they could truly have.

Shirt and pants put to rights, Erin sat beside him. She glanced at him for a moment before looking away. But then she reached out and took his hand, twining their fingers together.

One of them had to say something, and he was the officer. "This is—"

"Don't." Erin cut him off. "We'll be in New York soon enough. We can..." She trailed off rather than complete the sentence.

Life was waiting for them back there. They had a full tank of gas, and they'd be home by midnight if they took off right now. Instead Gibson tugged on Erin's arm and pulled her close, until she was straddling him, fully clothed, but still close, still perfect.

He kissed her again, putting his heart into it and confessing all the words he couldn't say. He lost himself in it, heart thundering when Erin moaned and kissed him back, her fingers threading through his hair and holding him tight.

He wanted to keep her there all night, but before long the wailing howl of a passing semi truck startled them both, and they looked towards the road, barely visible down the dark path that led to the parking lot.

"We should get going," Erin said, though she didn't try and move.

He ran his hand down her spine one more time, memorizing the feel of her, fearing this might be his last taste. So he kissed her again, just in case.

"I'm driving," he said, putting as much alpha into the words as he could.

She laughed and slid off, kissing him on the forehead. "You wish."

She took the driver's seat and Gibson didn't argue. And as the car cut through the dark night, the worries he hadn't been thinking of began to creep up.

How had the magic found him if they'd removed the mark from Erin's back?

He almost said something, but decided to keep quiet. As long as they were vigilant, it would be fine. There was no need to burden Erin with more worry.

But it churned in his gut as the miles went by.

# CHAPTER THIRTEEN

A YAWN TORE OUT of Erin's mouth as she drove into the darkness, the car drifting ever so slightly to the right. She didn't yank the steering wheel back. With the size of the vehicle, she feared that might send them careening into a ditch on the opposite side of the road. They hadn't passed another car in at least twenty minutes. But they were in Pennsylvania now, getting ever closer to New York City.

Her headlights cut through the darkness, the trees on either side of the road hanging over them like strange sentinels. A staticky radio station was the only noise, other than the coughing hiccup of the engine. Gibson was quiet in the passenger seat.

And he had to be Gibson. Not Jericho. The closer

they got to home, the surer she became that she had to leave that name behind.

She yawned again.

"I think we're getting pretty close to the farm," she said, breaking the silence between them. Gibson owned property in rural Pennsylvania that was perfect for the pack to run on as wolves. They got out there multiple times a month. And, perhaps most importantly, there were beds there. She and Gibson could sleep and regroup and then finish their journey in the morning.

Gibson grunted, and for a second she thought that was the only response she would get. But then he nodded. "Sounds good. I could use the sleep."

Gibson looked at the directions on their map and Erin was right in their estimate. About thirty minutes later they were pulling into the tiny town that was little more than a gas station, a pizza place, and a bunch of large farms. If they had a cell phone, Erin would have called ahead to place their order. Instead, she pulled into the parking lot of the pizza joint and sent Gibson inside to order at the counter.

The separation was necessary. Erin needed to put space between them, to remind herself that she was her own person who was perfectly capable of sitting in a car for fifteen minutes with no one else beside her.

But it was dark out, even with the bright light of the moon. In the shadows, she felt very jumpy. Were there dark magicians out there? Were they coming for her? Her fears had been growing with every mile of their journey. She was still shaken by the attack on Gibson, and she was trying not to show it. If he could be strong, so could she.

By the time he got back to the car, she banished those thoughts to the deep recesses of her mind. They had no place here.

The pizza smelled good and made her stomach rumble. By the time they got to the farm, they didn't bother getting out plates. Instead, they set the box on the counter and tore into it, devouring it like starving people in a matter of minutes.

The food made her feel a bit more human, or a bit more... shifter? Erin didn't like to waste a lot of time considering the implications her wolf form had on her humanity. Whatever it was, she was still a person.

"I could use a shower," she said, reaching for a napkin and wiping a bit of grease off her fingers.

Gibson flipped the empty box shut. "I'm going to

try and call someone in the city. Let them know what's going on."

In the shower, Erin let the hot water run over her body until she was pink and nearly scalded. It felt good, maybe too good. The water pressure at the farm was to die for, and without the rest of the pack there, she wasn't going to run out of hot water.

But as the water cascaded down her body, it was all too easy to remember the feel of Gibson's hands on her skin, his lips pressed against hers. Her fingers trailed down her body, teasing her most sensitive parts until she ripped her hand away.

No. She wasn't doing that here.

The journey was almost over. She and Gibson had to go back to being... whatever they were supposed to be. He couldn't be her mate. No matter how much her inner wolf insisted that was exactly who he was to her.

She turned the temperature down, perhaps in a bit of self-punishment, and quickly finished the shower.

Since the pack came out here often, all of them left some clothes in the guest rooms, and Erin was able to pull on a pair of sweats that fit properly and an old top that she had thought she lost in the laundry.

She was tempted to crawl into bed and hide away until morning. If she didn't go out there and talk to Gibson, there was no way to give in to temptation.

But she had never been a coward.

When she left the guest room, she found Gibson standing in a pair of low-slung sweats and nothing else. She had to bite her tongue to keep from making a sound and intentionally look at the wall over his shoulder to keep from ogling him.

He was a monster. A demon. Maybe an incubus, come to tempt her. But whatever it was, it really wasn't fair that he could stand there and look like that, and she wasn't supposed to touch him.

"I thought we could go for a run," he suggested. "Moon's bright tonight."

A run. Yes. That was exactly what she needed.

There was something routine in heading downstairs to where the sliding glass door let out into the backyard with the woods beyond. Gibson had it set up with a sensor pad, so they could close the door behind them and open it back up even when they were in their wolf forms. She chose to shift while still inside, using the privacy of one of the downstairs guest bedrooms to keep him from seeing her naked. Of course, he had seen the show before. But at this point, Erin had to do whatever she could to protect her heart.

She met Gibson outside and took a moment to admire the grace of his wolf form. They were a bit bigger than natural wolves, but that was the only difference. Gibson stood as if he had been born a wolf, the form as natural on him as anything else.

They took off running, and Erin knew this game. There was a stream through the woods about a mile or so away, and she and her packmates loved to race. Gibson's legs were longer than hers, and he could eat up the distance like it was nothing, but she was quick and right on his tail. She overtook him, letting out a bark of pleasure as the stream came into view.

Then a heavy body tackled her, and she rolled to the side, hitting a patch of mud and growling at Gibson's retreating form as he hit the stream first and won the race. Erin got back to her paws and shook off, letting the mud fly.

She growled at Gibson and took a threatening step forward. He was bigger than her and stronger than her, and that was as true in their wolf forms as in their human forms.

She did not give a single fuck. He didn't get to cheat and win.

Erin lunged at him, snapping her teeth playfully and taunting him until he met her.

It wasn't a fight, not really. But they were wolves. And the line between playing and fighting was always thin. She could feel his teeth in her fur, and it made her want to laugh, even if she didn't quite have the physical structure for that at the moment.

They might have stayed like that all night, fighting for dominance in a game that didn't really count. Gibson was the alpha, they both knew it. But at the moment, they were equal.

A scent drifted through the forest and they both froze, looking down the path to where the moonlight illuminated a proud buck, antlers gleaming in the moonlight.

There was no need for talking. Gibson took off, Erin right on his heels. They raced through the forest, and the buck realized it before long. They could bring the beast down, their wolfish instincts clamoring at them to do it.

But the buck got lucky. Either he knew some trick of the forest, or possibly she and Gibson just weren't dedicated enough, because before long the buck disappeared, and it was just the two of them lingering at the edge of the farm.

Erin couldn't bring herself to feel disappointed. She was still sated from the pizza, and there was no need to bring death and destruction to some family of deer tonight.

Slowly, she and Gibson padded back to the entrance to the farmhouse and headed inside, shifting from wolf to human as quickly as possible and each of them pulling on the bathrobes that they kept right next to the door inside the house so they wouldn't be stuck naked for long.

Erin knew she shouldn't look at Gibson. Even in a bathrobe, he would be temptation personified.

The air was charged between them, as if a veil of desire hung in the space separating their bodies. Inexorably, Erin's gaze was drawn to Gibson, her heart pounding like the drums of war in her chest.

It wouldn't take anything to close the distance between them and capture his mouth with her own. She could still feel the imprint of his fingers on her thighs, remembered the way his mouth had moved while she sat over him.

"Good run," she forced out, the words practically impersonal. "I'm going to bed." She didn't add that she was going alone, but that was obvious enough.

There were plenty of guest rooms in the house, but Erin chose the one upstairs and tried not to think about it too much. Gibson was the only member of the pack with a permanent room, and Erin could easily put more distance between them by taking one of the downstairs guest rooms.

She didn't.

She changed into her pajamas and got under the covers, wrapping the blanket tighter around her, even if it was a little too warm. Without Gibson beside her the empty bed feel almost intolerable, as if she hadn't been sleeping in a bed all by herself for a very long time. She clutched the blanket tighter, and tried to pretend it was Gibson's arm.

There was no way to pretend. He was a solid wall behind her, the kind of presence that couldn't be ignored. Or replicated.

Erin squeezed her eyes shut, trying to force her body into sleep.

She was in a comfortable bed, so she was basically safe. And yet, she had an easier time sleeping when she was tied up and held prisoner than when she was ten feet away from her mate.

In the darkness of her bedroom, she couldn't ignore who he was to her. She couldn't ignore the way her body cried out for him and the nearly impossible-to-ignore pull that wanted her to cross the house and go to his bedroom where she could sleep in his arms. That was all she needed, sleep. Nothing more.

Erin threw the covers off of her and sat up, gathering her knees close and clutching them as she leaned against the wall and gritted her teeth against the need to go to Gibson. She was fine. She was a grown up. She could sleep alone. And if she couldn't sleep, she could sit in the room until morning and suffer in silence.

The plan didn't appeal to her. She didn't really want to do it. She wanted Gibson so much that she had to actually fight back tears as her body tried to force her out of that bed. Her mind had to be stronger. One of them had to be strong. One of them had to put up the boundary and refuse to cross it.

They needed to talk about this. Come morning, they would be returning back to the pack, back to their old life. And they had to figure out how they would do that after everything that had happened between them.

A sound tickled her ears, and her heartbeat sped up, thinking Gibson was coming to find her. But it was just the sound of the TV in the other room, in the living room. "Fuck it." Erin eased herself off the bed and headed out to the living room, where she saw Gibson sitting on the couch, remote in his hand, the TV tuned to some competition reality show.

"Couldn't sleep?" she asked.

He shrugged. "Something like that."

Erin hesitated for a moment. She could still go back to her room. She could grab a drink from the kitchen, pretend that was why she came out. Or perhaps ask Gibson to turn the volume down. That wasn't what she wanted. She couldn't have what she really wanted. But she could have some small imitation of it, the diet soda of emotional longing.

She sat on the couch, careful to keep an entire cushion between them. She tried to concentrate on the show, judging the ingredients one of the chefs was using as if she had some sort of skill in the kitchen, but it was a losing battle. The magnetic pull between her and Gibson was something she had to physically fight, even as she found her body leaning closer and closer until she brushed up against his arm.

"Erin..." He murmured it softly, his breath ghosting over her ear.

Erin let out a shaky breath. "Please, don't." She didn't know what else to say.

But Gibson settled back against the couch, not making another move. After a moment, he reached out and grabbed her hand, gently squeezing it, offering her the contact that she couldn't help but need even as she knew she should fight it.

Exhaustion weighed on her, and she found herself relaxing into Gibson, her head slowly finding its way to his lap, where he lightly brushed his fingers against her hair. Her eyelids grew heavy, and she drifted to sleep, lulled by Gibson's steady presence.

If she dreamed, she didn't know what it was about.

She slowly rose back to consciousness, her body a little too hot and in a strange position, but with the comforting presence of Gibson right next to her.

She knew she should jerk away, should get up and put as much space between them, physical and emotional, as possible. But Erin was comfortable, even if there was a little slight ache in her neck, and she wanted to drift back to sleep.

She might have, except that Owen Myers burst through the front door, and when he saw them, he started cursing up a storm.

# CHAPTER FOURTEEN

Gibson couldn't hide in his bedroom all morning. He could smell freshly brewed coffee and hear the murmur of voices that rose to a roar and ebbed every few moments. If he was prone to imagining things, he might think he was in a restaurant instead of his farm.

But, no, that wasn't it. The entire pack had descended.

Owen was their vanguard, waking up Gibson and Jackson with his cheerful cursing. And Gibson was trying not to think about the knowing grin Owen had shot him before Gibson retreated to get dressed.

Owen's mate, Stasia, had come with him, as had her sister, Em, and Andre, Em's mate. And a few minutes later, everyone else had piled in: Vi and Rowe, Vega and Kerry, and finally, Hunter, the only unmated wolf in the pack.

No. Gibson shook his head. He wasn't mated. Jackson wasn't mated. Hunter wasn't the only one.

*Liar.*

He leaned against his dresser and gripped the lip so tightly he worried he might crack it. Gibson was not mated. Erin—Jackson—wasn't his. And now the entire pack was back together, and they had to go back to being how they always were.

Friends. Co-workers. Professionals.

He hated it.

He wanted to put his mark on her for all to see, to proclaim to the world that Erin Jackson was his and that he was hers and no one could tear them apart. The instinct was strong enough that he had to suppress a growl. He might have asked the others in the pack if what they'd felt was anything like this, but he couldn't.

He had to lead.

And there was no more hiding.

Jackson slipped out of the guest room beside his bedroom at the same moment he did and their gazes met. They shared a wry smile before she nodded down the short hallway towards the kitchen.

Vacation was over. If a rescue mission that involved being chased by evil witches counted as a vacation.

Now that Jackson was back and officially safe, it was as if a great weight had been lifted off the pack. Everyone was smiling, the heavy cloud of tension had cleared, and there was no longer the sense of doom that bad news might come and shatter them at any second.

As Jackson led the way to the kitchen, Gibson almost reached out. He wanted to run his fingers down her back, to remind himself that she was there, that she was his, and that everything would be alright.

But she wasn't his, and Gibson kept his hands to himself.

The din quieted to a dull roar when they joined, and Owen shot Jackson a grin, eyebrows waggling. That urge to growl came again, but Gibson suppressed it. Taking Owen by the throat and demanding he show a bit of respect would only make things worse.

And confirm what everyone was pretending they didn't know.

"If you wanted a vacation, Jackson, you could have just said," Owen said, ignoring the mental daggers Gibson was throwing his way. "No need to be so dramatic."

"I guess we can't all be so annoying that the evil witches refuse to keep us captive," Jackson shot back as she grabbed a coffee mug and poured a cup for Gibson before making one for herself.

That got a laugh from Owen, Andre, and Rowe. Kerry was the newest member of their pack, and she'd been closely involved in the op that saw Owen kidnapped. And it was Kerry's own abduction that had led to Jackson's. Her face was carefully schooled to neutrality.

Vi wasn't smiling, not quite, but she rolled her eyes at her mate when he said something quietly.

Gibson was glad they were all here. No matter his earlier frustration, no matter that he wanted to suck up as much time alone with Jackson as possible. These people were his family, people he hadn't quite chosen but who'd stuck together through some supremely weird shit and made it out the other side.

If he was going to war, he couldn't hope for a better army.

Hunter gave him a tight smile and stood. "If we're going to hang out here, we need some food," she said. "I can do a run." It was normally her responsibility to pick up the pizza, and Gibson knew Hunter got a bit squirrelly in the big crowd.

"We'll go with," Kerry volunteered, grabbing Vega's hand.

Bryan Vega shrugged.

Good. Gibson didn't want any of his pack alone right now, not until the threat against them was neutralized. But his stomach growled, and Hunter had a point.

There were good natured shouts from the rest of the pack requesting food they all knew the small grocery store in town absolutely didn't have. Where could you even get alligator jerky in rural Pennsylvania?

Jackson took the seat vacated by Hunter and Gibson took Vega's, leaving an empty chair between them. It was for the best, they needed the space.

"Give us a rundown of what happened when you were taken," Gibson told Jackson, the instruction a bit more curt than necessary. But he couldn't modulate his voice, not if he didn't want to put his entire heart into it.

"Yeah, where'd you find that old station wagon?" Owen asked, "I'm pretty sure it's older than me. Hell, it might be older than Gibson."

Gibson ignored him. "Start at the beginning." He

and Jackson had been so focused on getting home...
and other things... that she hadn't given him much
of a report. Now, with most of the pack together, it
was time.

Jackson gripped her coffee mug tight and stared
at the surface of the beverage. Gibson had to curl his
hand into a fist under the table to keep from
reaching out to offer her comfort.

Her tongue darted out to lick her lips and she
began. "We were on the mission to recover Kerry. I
got hit with something and it knocked me out.
Didn't feel like a weapon. Maybe a spell?" She
glanced over at Vi, who nodded at the possibility.
"Then I woke up on a ship. I tried to escape once, but
there were at least four men holding me captive.
One of them had this device and he could control me
with it."

Owen made a noise low in his throat, and
everyone looked at him. "We saw something like
with Stasia's brother. He had a thing that let him
control shifters. Control us."

Jackson nodded. Her face was blank, her tone
even, but Gibson could feel the strain coming off of
her, and there was no way to take the pain away.

"The next time I woke up, I was alone. I

managed to sneak off the ship and swim to shore. I stole a car and called Gibson. He came to get me."

"And no one thought to call us?" Surprisingly, that came from Andre, who normally kept his cool.

Jackson didn't respond to that.

"Here's where we need Vi's help," Jackson said, explaining about the mark on her back and their difficulty with phones. "I think I was able to call Gibson because I was still covered in salt water. I remember you saying something about that disrupting magic. Does that sound right?"

Vi pursed her lips and thought for a moment. "Could be. Or they needed to do something to activate the spell and hadn't yet realized you were gone. A spell like that takes a good dose of power to keep the connection or reestablish it if it breaks. Never heard of someone using sharpie before. Usually you'd use henna, or maybe charcoal if it didn't need to last long."

"They found us again after we removed the mark." Gibson could still feel the oppressive shadow of that thing pressing down on him. He fucking hated magic. "Any ideas?"

"Do you mind if I take a look at you?" Vi asked Jackson. "There might be something you missed."

Jackson got up, and Vi followed her towards the

guest room. Gibson lasted all of five seconds before he followed after, leaving Owen, Andre, Rowe, Stasia, and Em at the table to share knowing glances.

Gibson had to ignore that. He'd do this for anyone in his pack.

He slipped into the guest room behind Vi and shut the door as Jackson slipped off her top and bra, showing Vi her back. There was nothing there but smooth skin, not even a hint of the mark that had dogged them.

Vi raised a hand, and it glowed faintly. "I'm going to touch you," she warned Jackson.

Gibson bit back a growl. Vi was their witch. She was Rowe's mate. She could be trusted.

But magic had already harmed Jackson once.

Vi placed her fingers against Jackson's shoulder, and Jackson flinched. This time the growl escaped, and Gibson stepped forward. But instead of disrupting Vi, all he did was take Erin's hand. She shot him a small smile, and it did something to settle his wolf.

Vi said nothing, but the witch saw everything. At the moment, Gibson didn't care.

The witch made a humming sound and ran her fingers over the area where the mark had been. He couldn't be sure, but she seemed to outline it exactly.

Not a great sign.

"There's something here," Vi murmured. "It's faint, but there's a whisper of a connection. I'm going to need to do a spell to trace it back to its source and to sever it."

"Yes, do it." Erin's voice had an edge of desperation. "Now, please."

Vi made an apologetic sound. "I need to get some supplies first. They might be expensive." That was to him.

Gibson nodded. "Anything you need."

She nodded and patted Jackson's shoulder. "We need to do this soon, before the connection strengthens again." She let go of Jackson and slipped out of the room.

Gibson bared his teeth. No evil witch was going to touch Erin. He'd tear them apart before they got close.

# CHAPTER FIFTEEN

WHEN HAD the room got so small? Erin was pretty sure the walls were closing in. Even the cotton of her stretchy shirt threatened to squeeze her tight until she couldn't move. The air around her was too heavy, like she was breathing through a thick blanket of smog that had settled over the room.

Gibson lay a hand on her shoulder, the heat from his touch radiating deep into her skin where Vi's magicky fingers had left an invisible imprint over the faded magical marking. "She's got this," Gibson said, voice heavy with reassurance. "There's no witch I'd trust more."

Erin turned towards him and his hand fell away. "Because we know so many witches." Every witch they knew came through Vi, not that it was a bad thing. Erin trusted her. Vi was as much a part of the pack as anyone.

But her nerves were getting to her.

"I can hunt down Glinda the Good if you want. No one else is putting their hands on you." There was a pause after he said it.

Erin let it stretch. "And if I wanted that..." It wasn't quite a question. She wasn't brave enough to really ask.

"Then I guess we're going to Oz." Their eyes met. Gazes locked. Gibson's blue eyes blazed in the dim light of the room.

She took a deep breath, her skin faintly tingling, both from the magic and from Gibson's intensity. "That's not what I meant."

Gibson reached out and tipped up her chin. He ran his thumb over her lips, and they were so sensitive it made her shiver. Erin closed her eyes, relishing the sensation. She leaned in towards him, the tension between them so thick she could barely breathe.

She could feel the heat of his body, smell the faint aroma of soap mingling with his natural scent. She opened her mouth to speak, but couldn't find the words to say more.

She wanted to kiss him more than she wanted

her next sunrise. Desire surged through her veins, urging her closer to him. It wouldn't take anything to lean in and capture his lips with her own. She remembered the taste of him, the way his tongue felt when it tangled with hers, the way he could light her body up until she was an inferno of bliss.

But they weren't kissing each other anymore. She didn't need a conversation to know that.

Erin stepped back.

If she started kissing Gibson, she wouldn't stop. Especially not with a bed conveniently two feet away from them. It wouldn't take anything to wrap her arms around him and stumble back into the mattress, letting their clothes fall by the wayside. Her arms ached to wrap around his neck and tumble into the bed and let worries and regrets fall by the wayside, at least until morning.

Her body tightened in desire, and from the unsteady breath Gibson pulled in, he knew it too. If the pack weren't right outside, Erin would throw caution to the wind.

If.

"I want you to go with Vi to get the supplies," Gibson said, all business, as if they weren't a breath away from crashing into one another.

"I'm safer here." *With you.* That part she wasn't

brave enough to speak. But Gibson's farm had its own kind of magic about it, though it wasn't supernatural. It was the kind that came from the absolute certainty that no one would bother them as long as this place belonged to Gibson.

But even that was a facade.

"You're safer with a witch." Gibson's voice grew firm. "Your presence here could put the rest of the pack in danger if we're discovered. Vi can protect you."

"I can protect myself." Anger flared hot at the idea she needed to be sheltered.

"Is that so?" A challenge underlay his words.

"I got off that boat myself, didn't I? No help there. Not even when—" She choked back the memories that threatened to flood, things she'd rather not consider. "I handled it."

"Go with Vi," Gibson commanded, voice firm as steel. There was no or else. There didn't need to be.

He stomped out of the room and Erin stayed, just for a few more seconds. She needed to get her bearings. But no matter how much she wanted to hide away, she wouldn't allow it. She didn't hide, not from Gibson, not from anyone.

Vi was waiting at the front of the house and

scowling at the rusty station wagon. "I'm not sure how that thing made it here without falling apart."

Erin ran a finger over the hood. "She's stronger than she looks. She'll outlast all of us."

Vi laughed. "Now I'm sure you've gone insane. Did you need something else?"

"Gibson wants me to go with you." She didn't look back at the house, and she tried to keep her tone even. Everything was fine.

Vi shrugged and nodded toward her black sedan. "Let's get going, then. It's early, but the place should be open. Their clientele really likes morning."

"So this isn't some vampire den or whatever?" The surprises of the magical world were unending, and at a certain point, Erin had decided just to roll with it.

That startled another laugh out of the witch. "Vampires? No. Basically the opposite, really."

Erin pondered what that could mean as she slid into the passenger seat of Vi's car. Music from a streaming station was their soundtrack on the drive. It was different than with Gibson, mainly the lack of simmering attraction threatening to bubble to the surface at any moment. But Vi knew how to share a silence, and Erin appreciated that.

After a half hour or so, they pulled into a parking

lot. "Here?" Erin peered at the building, wondering if she was missing something. "An antique shop? How is this the opposite of vampires? Are vampires even real?"

Vi shot her a look like Erin was the crazy one for asking that, and she rolled her eyes when it was clear Erin meant it. "Yeah, of course. And old people love this stuff. They're the opposite of vampires."

Erin wasn't sure that made sense, but who was she to argue? "So is there a secret magic shop in the back? A portal? Why here?"

Vi led her into the store and walked with purpose to a table full of old lamps. "No special store. Spells aren't really like recipes where we need eye of newt or whatever... at least, not all of them. I'm building resonance for this casting, and antiques are absolutely loaded with latent magic. It's that extra bit of oomph you can't really get from a lamp from Target." She picked up an old lamp with a red shade ringed in yellow fringe and shoved it to Erin.

"I absolutely agree!" An older man clapped his hands together, drawing Erin and Vi's attention. He was wearing a button-up plaid shirt with bright green suspenders and dark purple pants. His hair was the flat black that came from dye, but dye couldn't hide the deep lines around his eyes that put him closer to sixty rather than fifty. "I'm Gregory and this is my shop. That's a wonderful piece."

Had he heard them talking about magic? Erin didn't know what was worse, confirming for this man that magic was real or agreeing that the war crime of a lamp she was holding was wonderful.

"I've been known to take a piece here and there for my coven. We just did the most amazing harvest ritual." He picked up a plate shaped like a corn cob and handed it to Vi. "What do you think?"

"Shouldn't a harvest ritual happen before the harvest?" Erin wasn't much of a farmer, but it was getting late into fall.

Gregory gave her a tight smile and turned back to Vi. "What do you practice? Gardnerian? Alexandrian? My coven is a bit more eclectic. And I've been looking into Reiki. It's so nice to meet a fellow practitioner!"

Vi shot Erin a desperate look, but Erin just shook her head. The witch was on her own. If Erin opened her mouth, she was going to burst out laughing.

"Actually I'm looking for just a few more things, could you help me?" Vi's voice was strained, but she managed to distract Gregory for long enough that they retrieved a tarnished silver necklace with a blue glass gem. Erin didn't touch that one. Shifter skin didn't like silver. And Vi finished it off with an old tin coffee can for a brand Erin didn't recognize. The mascot was a vaguely terrifying man with a rictus grin and a hand full of what appeared to be rocks. Maybe coffee beans?

Gregory tried to invite Erin to his next coven meeting, but Erin had to decline, and once they were back in the car and safely on the road, they both burst out laughing.

"Should I tell Rowe?" Erin asked between gasps of laughter. "Is he going to be jealous?"

"You can't tell him!" Her hands gripped the steering wheel tight, voice going up an octave. "I get to tell him first! Oh god." She gasped again, and eventually her breathing evened out.

"You find a lot of people like that?" Erin had spent the better part of the last three years trying desperately to hide what she was. The fact that a self-described Wiccan could meet a real-life witch and not even pause to consider real magic blew her mind.

"More than you'd think." Vi adjusted the radio settings to turn the sound down. "Make sure you keep all that stuff in your lap. I need it to absorb some of your energy."

Erin clutched the lamp, coffee can, and necklace,

her arm a little strained but not too bad. "For real? I think you're making this up."

"Half of magic is making things up."

Erin didn't put the stuff down. The drive crawled by, mysteriously seeming to take longer than it had to get to the antique shop. And anxiety bit at her heels. Vi hadn't said anything about Gibson, but she had to realize something was going on. Everyone did.

By now Owen had probably twisted the story of finding them napping on the couch into walking in on them in flagrante. And it wasn't like he was that far off.

"Are you—" Erin bit back the words, but not before a couple escaped her traitorous mouth.

Vi quirked up an eyebrow, but only spared a quick glance, too focused on the road.

Erin slumped back, letting her head thump against the headrest. "Me and Gibson."

The witch hummed in the back of her throat, acknowledgment rather than agreement.

Erin waited several more seconds, but Vi clearly wasn't going to show pity. "Are you judging? I know it shouldn't have happened." Her inner wolf growled at those words. She and her beast were not in agreement about that part.

"Why not?" asked Vi.

"He's an officer, and my boss, and I know he cares about the age thing, but that's not a big deal." Saying it now felt... light. Insubstantial. Like she and Gibson had been trying to get around a mountain only to find that the entire thing had been made of cotton candy the entire time.

Vi glanced at her before quickly looking back at the road. "He's not an officer anymore. The boss thing is only as complicated as you let it be, and he's your mate. What's to question?"

Mate. Her mind had been circling around the word for days. For much longer than that, if she was honest. "You can't know that." How could Vi be sure when Erin wasn't?

The witch scoffed. "It's a magical connection, isn't it? I didn't say anything before because it wasn't my place. But it's as strong as I've ever seen it before. That bond isn't going to fade anytime soon. Not unless you take drastic measures."

Erin's inner wolf growled before she could ask what kind of drastic measures Vi was talking about. She shifted in her seat, and the antiques in her lap clinked against each other. Drastic measures didn't matter. It was far too late to walk away now.

## CHAPTER SIXTEEN

Gibson felt like he was standing in a fucking fairy tale. Green plants sprouted all around him, bees buzzing between flowers, butterflies dancing in the air, and ticks no doubt ready to burrow into any bit of unprotected skin.

He glared down at a butterfly that had landed on the leaf of a small yellow flower and tried to convince himself that his sour mood had nothing to do with the distance between him and Jackson.

She was fine. She was with a witch and more than protected. The threat against her was hundreds of miles away. Everything was alright.

And still, the wolf that lived inside him grumbled.

Gibson shook off some of the worry. What he

and the rest of the pack were doing right now would help Jackson more than sitting around and brooding. Vi needed herbs and flowers for her spell. Gibson could help gather those.

But what the hell did wild ginger even look like?

Purple wildflowers he could figure out. They were little purple flowers. He already had a bunch in his hand and was tempted to skip through the woods as if he was on his way to his grandmother's house. Too bad he was the big bad wolf.

"All good?" Rowe approached him, carrying a small plastic tote that was already bursting with plants. Gibson dumped his own flowers into it.

"Seems like we've got plenty."

Rowe grinned. "You'd think that. But Vi goes through enough of this crap that it might be cheaper to just open up a flower shop to keep her supplied. I think we're good on the wild flowers now, but we could use more of the ginger."

"The only ginger I know is back in the kitchen. Tell me what I'm looking for." He tried not to growl it out, tried to be reasonable. But he only had so much resolve.

Gibson's ire had no effect on Rowe. He didn't know how the witch could stand being mated to the guy.

Rowe crouched down next to a bunch of green leaves that looked pretty much like everything else Gibson had been looking at. "Do you see these pointed leaves? Kind of like a circular triangle."

"A circular triangle? Really?" But when Gibson looked at where he was pointing, he—unfortunately—understood where the guy was coming from. "Yeah, I see."

"There's some flowers in here too. They're a reddish purple. It's okay if we don't have a ton, but Vi will want some." He plucked one of the flowers and showed it to Gibson.

Gibson nodded. "Weird red flowers, coming up."

For a few minutes, they plucked ginger and added it to Rowe's container. It lulled Gibson into a false sense of security, and he didn't sense the attack until Rowe spoke.

"How was the drive up? You and Erin seemed healthy." His tone was completely even. Almost polite, really.

But Gibson had known the man long enough to hear the layers. He glared at his packmate and tore extra ginger from the ground.

"Hey! Watch the roots! We're not weeding the forest."

"Take your leaves and go," Gibson said. He

wasn't going to spend the afternoon talking about his feelings with a bunch of meddling soldiers. They gossiped like no one's business, and his private life wasn't fodder for their conversations.

Rowe wandered away, and Gibson took a different path in the woods, looking for more of the ginger. A few minutes later, Andre came up to him and crouched beside him, plucking at leaves.

"Shouldn't you be working with your mate?" he asked. Everyone was fanned out in the woods: Owen and Stasia, Rowe, Kerry and Vega, Hunter, and Em, who Andre had apparently left alone.

"She's helping Stasia," he said. "They kicked me out of the club. Apparently it's sister time."

"Uh huh." Andre and Owen's mates were half-sisters and had already been close before they found out about werewolves. Now they were thicker than thieves. He wouldn't be shocked if one day Stasia and Em forced their mates to move into one giant house so they could spend even more time together.

Andre plucked at something that Gibson was almost certain wasn't ginger before looking at him slyly. "Owen was telling me—"

"Think really hard about if you want to finish that sentence." Teasing was part of their life, their world, but Gibson still had to wrap his head around... everything. He could take it with the best of them, but he had to find stable ground first.

Owen walked up, crunching on every leaf in the forest and probably scaring away any wildlife. How the man could call himself a wolf, Gibson would never know. "Hey—"

"No." Whatever it was, Gibson would shove all the wild ginger he could find into Owen's mouth before he let him ask even one question.

Owen cackled.

Something rumbled in the distance, and Gibson tilted his head, trying to hear better. A train? But they were a few miles from the nearest tracks. Close enough to hear the wailing of the horns, but rarely the rumble of the cars.

Whatever it was, it came from the house.

And it was growing stronger.

Gibson dropped his ginger and ran towards the house. He'd just broken through the clearing when a fireball ignited and sent him flying off his feet.

The last thing he saw was the wreckage of the station wagon.

# CHAPTER SEVENTEEN

The scene was chaos as Vi pulled the car into Gibson's driveway. Acrid smoke bit at Erin's nose, her eyes watering, even with the windows up. She clutched the items in her lap tightly, as if they might spontaneously explode, before carefully setting them down near her feet.

Running towards danger without assessing the situation was a quick way to get yourself killed.

She was careful as she got out of the car, taking things in. Vi had a hand up in front of herself, the air faintly glowing as the witch did some kind of magic. Kerry was next to the remains of the station wagon, fire extinguisher in hand as her red hair whipped around her face, tossed by a wind Erin couldn't feel.

Vega was next to her, using a large blanket to try

and smother the rest of the flames. The entire pack seemed to be there, working together to put out the fire... except...

At the side of the house, nearly obscured from view, Stasia was bent over someone, her expression fierce, the same one Erin was sure she would have seen if she'd ever encountered Stasia back when the woman worked in the ER.

And though she was far away, though he was laying on the ground and mostly out of sight, Erin knew exactly who Stasia was hovering over.

Erin took off running, not giving a single damn about anything but Gibson laying there on the ground, unmoving, with a doctor grimly looming over him.

"Jericho!" His name tore out of her, somewhere between a curse and a prayer. His first name might have turned a few heads. Erin didn't care. She skidded to a halt, dropped to her knees, and stared at him, willing him to be alright.

His face was screwed up in pain, but his eyes were open and he was glaring at something she couldn't see.

"It's just a twisted ankle," Stasia was telling him. "Looks like you tripped when the car exploded. Just baby it for a bit. It will be fine."

Stasia gave Erin a nod and then was on her feet and heading toward the rest of the pack to check for injuries.

Erin threw her arms around Gibson and held him tight, breathing his scent in deep, as if it was the only thing strong enough to prove to her that he was okay, that he was right there with her.

"What happened?" she asked. It was kind of obvious. A car was blasted to smithereens. But her mind felt a bit sluggish, like everything was moving through molasses, her thoughts not quite able to coalesce into anything that made sense.

Gibson's arms were solid around her, his own face buried in her neck, his lips rubbing against her, not quite a kiss, but something just as intense. "Do you think Hammond's insurance covers magical explosions?"

That startled a laugh out of Erin. Her fingers brushed the hair at the back of his neck and she slid her hand up until she cradled the back of his head. Gibson pulled back just enough to look at her, eyes intense.

Everyone was around them. They were probably looking. Erin didn't give two shits.

She kissed him, right there, in the broad daylight, like neither of them had a care in the world. It was a simple thing, of lips and only the slightest hint of tongue.

But it had her inner wolf purring in satisfaction.

*Mate.*

Yes. Okay. Maybe. She didn't care what he was, as long as he was hers.

It took a few minutes to convince herself to let him go so he could stand up. Gibson had a slightly dazed look on his face that she didn't think had anything to do with the explosion.

Once on her feet, Erin offered him a hand up, which he took. And he didn't drop it once he was steady.

No one said a thing as they joined Vi, who leaned over the largest part of the wreck, her hands glowing with lavender magic. It made the hair on Erin's forearms stand up and she could almost hear something staticky in her ears, like when the TV was on but the screen remained blank.

Vi curled her hands into fists and the lavender glow disappeared. She stumbled, but Rowe was there to catch her, one arm going around her shoulders as she leaned against her mate's side.

Erin squeezed Gibson's fingers. He squeezed back.

Vi nodded at her mate and regained her footing.

"Magic did this. Some part of the spell that was attached to Erin hooked itself to the car. It took awhile to accumulate enough power for this, but when it did... boom."

Doing the math in her head, Erin tried to figure out if they might have still been driving in that thing if they'd continued on to New York. Or, if they'd parked it in the garage in Brooklyn, it might have killed them all, and taken out a good portion of the neighborhood.

"Was it a warning?" Gibson asked. "Why trigger it when no one was close enough to get hurt?"

Her heartbeat had barely calmed down from seeing him lying on the ground. Bile rose in Erin's throat as she considered what might have happened if he'd been three feet closer when it blew.

"I think that was just luck," Vi responded, to growls and grumbles from the pack. "What I suspect was done to the car is dangerous because it can't be controlled. A witch put her intention into this spell and just let it go."

"Did the magic spread when the car exploded?" Owen asked, and everyone looked his way. "What?" His chest puffed out a bit. "I can't have magic questions?"

"It's not a bad thing to ask," Vi said, before

someone could start teasing. She'd been with them long enough to know to cut things off at the head. "But, no. The spell burnt up all the magic in the car. We're safe from that. But I'm going to set up wards around the house, just in case I missed something. There's a small chance someone might have tied a tracking spell to the magic in the car. It would be a bit complex, so it's not likely, but I don't want to take a chance."

"Do you want us confined to the house?" Gibson asked.

The whole pack, mates and all, would make it a tight fit, but they would manage. It couldn't be worse than the barracks.

"I'll set the spell to encompass the front yard and the back yard to the tree line. But no one can go for a run. I can't cover all that property if I'm going to keep my power for later." Vi gave Erin a grimacing smile. "This will take a few hours, but I think we need to do it before I check the magic on your back."

Erin nodded. "It's your call. You're the magic expert." She tried not to let any disappointment show. Every time she thought of the mark, her skin felt like ants were crawling all over it, but the protection of the pack had to come before her comfort.

"I'll go get my things," Vi said, turning and heading towards the house. Rowe followed after her.

"Vega, Kerry, Hunter," Gibson said, taking control of the scene, "I want the three of you taking stock of the exterior of the house. Look for any damage. The rest of us are going to pick through as much of the wreckage as we can. I don't want anyone cutting a paw on gnarled metal during a run, so let's get this fixed now."

They split up in the assigned groups. Though the wreckage had flown quite a ways, Erin couldn't bring herself to stray too far from Gibson. They ended up dumping twisted pieces of old car right on top of the remains of the car's body, with Gibson saying he'd call in someone to haul it away once they'd dealt with everything else.

"Are you doing alright?" he asked between hauls, when they snuck inside for a quick drink of water.

"I could do without the evil magic," she admitted.

Gibson got a contemplative look on his face.

"What are you thinking?" She reached out and ran her thumb over the furrow between his eyes. Gibson trapped her wrist and tugged on it until her hand ended up cradling his cheek, the bristles of his stubble rough on her skin.

"I think the past couple of days haven't been all bad." He tilted his chin to the side to brush his lips against her palm.

She leaned in and kissed him quickly, darting away before it could turn into anything even worse. "No," she agreed. "Not all bad."

Someone cleared their throat behind them and they both startled, but they didn't break apart. Erin looked over her shoulder to see Rowe with a wide grin on his face. "Vi's ready for you."

# CHAPTER EIGHTEEN

"I thought you said the wards would only stretch to the trees," Gibson said as he followed her, Vi, and Rowe past the edge of the woods and onto a bit of the walking trail that was circled in candles with the lamp, necklace, and coffee can set equidistant from each other around the circle. Each item had three pieces of rough pink quartz in front of them and sat on a bed of flowers.

"We're outside the wards," the witch replied.

"Why?" Erin asked. She didn't like it. She wanted to shuffle her feet back until she was safely ensconced in Vi's magic where no evil witches could get to her. But she kept her mouth shut. She was a strong, independent shifter. She wasn't going to be afraid of a bit of forest.

"Magic," Rowe offered as he crouched over one of the candles to light it.

Erin glared at the man.

Vi ignored him. "If there's anything tying you back to the person who put that mark on you, we don't want to create a hole through the wards when we do the spell. It will weaken them and could give an enemy witch an easy target to break my spell when—if—she arrives. We're close enough that we can sprint for the wards if anything attacks, but that's unlikely. I've stretched my magic over the area to scan for any threats and nothing pinged."

"You can do that?" asked Gibson. "How does that work?"

Vi shrugged. "It's sort of like listening really hard for a specific sound. Gives me a headache if I do it for too long. But in times like these I give a listen, so to speak, once an hour or so." She turned to Erin. "Take off your top."

Rowe made a sound that might have turned into actual words if his mate hadn't glared at him.

Gibson growled and took a step in front of Erin. "You don't look," he warned.

"I've seen her naked before. Besides, my mate is a hot and terrifying witch. Sure, I can *see* Jackson, but I'm not looking."

Growly, possessive Gibson wasn't supposed to be so hot. Unfortunately, Erin's libido hadn't gotten that memo.

Erin turned to face Gibson and met his eyes. "It's okay," she said, and pulled her shirt over her head. She handed it to him. "Keep this safe for me?"

He took it from her and held it carefully, as if it was precious.

"You can keep your bra on," Vi offered. "I just need access to your shoulder."

Erin nodded, her skin pebbling a bit in the cool evening air. The sun hadn't quite set, but the forest was growing dark, the candles doing their best to fight off the encroaching night.

Rowe finished lighting the candles and stepped outside the circle. Vi looked at Gibson expectantly and nodded in approval when he stepped back as far as Rowe.

"This might tickle," Vi warned, and then something started to crawl around Erin's shoulder. It felt slimy and cold, like an octopus or something was using her shoulder as a playset. Erin tried not to flinch into it, but it made her gorge rise at the wrongness of the thing.

What kind of magic was Vi calling on? It couldn't be good.

She wanted to turn around to see what Vi was doing, as if she could make sense of any sort of arcane mastery that the witch brought forth. Instead, Erin rooted her feet in place and stared straight ahead. Gibson shifted his position until he was standing right in front of her, eyes boring into her.

Then his face cracked and he offered her a smile.

Oh fuck. She loved him.

Totally, completely, head over heels, never coming back from it, loved him. It was the kind of thing that had been lurking deep in her subconscious for so long that she couldn't quite be sure when it fully blossomed. But now the slimy sensation faded away until it might as well have just been her and Gibson, sharing a romantic, if strange, night in the woods.

She wanted a thousand nights like this. A million, even. However many she could grab and hold close, the darkness circling them and keeping them safe from anything that might try and tear them apart.

Erin's worries about the obstacles evaporated to nothing, and she felt like she could take a deep breath for the first time in ages. Gibson was hers. No going back. And no letting anything stand between them and happiness.

It was a good thought, a great thought, even. But it was overshadowed by a burst of light that had Gibson flinching back.

Erin spun around, no longer caring if Vi needed her facing outward. But Vi didn't seem to notice.

She was ensconced in a ball of light, purple and yellow and hints of red all swirling together to make it almost look like the witch was caught inside of a marble. She waved her arms around and the light moved with her. Her face was a mask of intensity that Erin could just see beyond the magic.

It had to take a ton of power to do... whatever it was Vi was doing.

What kind of strength would a witch who called on darker sources of power have?

Erin didn't want to consider it, but she was pretty sure they were going to find out.

The lamp, coffee can, and necklace all started to hover about two feet off the ground, wobbling a little but holding position. Dark blue light, difficult to make out in the dim of the forest, flowed from those antiques and into the swirling marble around Vi.

It blended together, looking a bit like a rolling

storm on a weather map, circling in one direction as Vi guided it, her body contorted as she called on more magic.

At least, that was what Erin thought was happening.

Her shoulder pricked again, and this time it wasn't slimy. It hurt. Needle pricks and fire ants and acid, all strong enough to make Erin gasp and curl her hand into a fist. But she forced herself to choke back any louder sound, to cloak the pain as best she could.

Who knew what might happen if Gibson broke the circle of magic around them? If he thought she was in pain, there was nothing that would stop him from crossing it to get to her.

Erin breathed through it, and either she got used to it or it started to fade. She wasn't quite sure which, but she could manage, and that was all that mattered.

White light started to form at the poles of the globe around Vi, slowly crawling down until it blotted out all the other colors and Vi was encircled completely in opaque whiteness.

For a breathless moment, everything came to a stand still, and even the pain in Erin's shoulder disappeared. Then the white around Vi flared so bright that it threatened to fry Erin's eyes, even when she squeezed them closed.

The light rushed over her, as strong as a wind, and then it faded. When Erin opened her eyes, Vi stared right at her, her own eyes taken over by the swirl of colors that had once surrounded her.

Vi opened her mouth and screamed, a tower of black smoke billowing out until she collapsed and the magic around them blinked out as if it had never been there at all. The candles went dark and Erin saw no sign of the antiques.

Rowe rushed forward and scooped his mate off the ground.

Vi blinked her eyes open and met Erin's gaze. "Run," she croaked out, leaning of out Rowe's embrace and pointing straight at Erin. "Run to the wards. Now!"

# CHAPTER NINETEEN

Gibson grabbed Erin out of the circle and shoved her towards the trail leading back to the house. She stumbled, but before he had to scoop her up and carry her, she got her feet under her and took off sprinting.

He was right behind her, with Rowe and Vi taking up the rear.

It felt like the entire forest was watching him, eyes that didn't belong. These were his woods. He was the biggest predator.

Tonight he felt like prey.

His ears popped as he crossed over the invisible line of Vi's magic. Erin slowed and glanced over her shoulder at him. Once Rowe and Vi crossed over, Vi doubled over, hands clenched on her knees, and sucked in deep breaths.

Rowe was a sentinel over her, rubbing her back reassuringly as his eyes scanned their surroundings for any threat.

Gibson handed Erin her shirt and she slipped it back on.

Vi stood back up. "Let's get inside," she said. "Everyone should hear this. I don't have the energy to say it twice."

There was a thick air of anticipation inside the house, and at least some of the tension released when the four of them got back inside. It was a full house. Gibson's place was big, but it wasn't built for eleven people.

Maybe once this was done, he'd think about constructing the extension he'd been considering for awhile.

The overstuffed chair in the corner was empty, and Gibson sat there. Erin sank down onto the arm of the chair and leaned against him. Rowe leaned against the wall behind Vi while everyone else got comfortable on the couch and the floor.

"What did you find?" Erin asked.

Vi let out a deep breath, her face grim. "I recognize the signature of the magic on you."

"That's a good thing, isn't it?" Gibson would rather face a known enemy than an unknown.

The witch shrugged, then glanced at her mate and then at Hunter. "Do you two remember Katrina Stevens? From the job where we all met?"

Gibson and Owen had been there, too. The pack had been hired to protect Vi's coven from another coven, but it had been a ruse. Vi's own coven leader, Rosalie Sutton, had been up to no good and had turned on them all before she was apprehended by a mysterious force of magic law enforcement that Gibson still didn't have much information on.

"I remember her," said Hunter from her spot on the floor. "Wasn't she in cahoots with Rosalie?"

Vi nodded. "She escaped. I haven't heard anything about her in months. The rest of the coven hasn't said a word. They act like Rosalie and her cronies are dead and we shouldn't speak of it at all." She shook her head, as if clearing away the cobwebs. "Katrina laid the original spell on Erin, I'm sure of it. I'd recognize the power signature anywhere."

"What does that mean for us?" That came from Erin, and her arm stretched to wrap around him and rest on his shoulder.

"It's nothing good," Vi confirmed. "Katrina

shouldn't have that much power. For the magic that was worked on you, that should have taken a full coven. I only sensed two other magical signatures mixed up with hers, and that power was minor." She glanced at Stasia. "I think this goes back to Rosalie and your brother." Then her gaze roved over the rest of the pack. "And back to how you all were turned in the first place."

Shock reverberated around the room, and Gibson straightened, a growl gathered in the back of his throat and ready to face an unseen threat. But that threat was long gone and far away. Three years ago and on another continent.

He still had occasional nightmares about it.

He'd been stationed in Germany, as had every other member of his now pack. None of them had known each other except in passing. Gibson's career had been on an upswing. He was looking at his next promotion, and at a possible command that would catapult him to great heights. He'd had plans.

And then someone had knocked him out and dragged him into a dark forest to perform darker magic, and he'd been forever changed, right along with Hunter, Owen, Andre, Erin, Rowe, and Vega.

In the time since, they'd been searching for

answers. Rosalie Sutton gave them their first big clue, and Vi and Rowe had been doing their research, but they'd run out of leads, and then Erin had been taken and all resources had gone into finding her.

"What do you mean?" It was Andre who asked it.

"Remember the dead shifters and witches?" Vi prompted. Rosalie had been involved in secret magic that killed supernatural beings. When Andre nodded, Vi continued. "We speculated that she was pulling power from them. It's old, dark magic. Super taboo. It's basically magical cannibalism." She shuddered.

Rowe stepped forward and wrapped his arms around her from behind. Vi sank into the embrace for a second before he let go, and then she took a deep breath and continued.

"It's also very obvious and very wasteful. You're left with a string of dead bodies, and it's pretty clear when someone's been drained of vital magic. And witches belong to covens. Shifters belong to packs. You can find the lone witch or wolf here and there, but eventually you'll run out and people will start looking for their friends. Unless you make your own power sources."

Em hesitantly raised her hand, index finger

pointing up while the rest curled into a fist. "Couldn't you just have a wolf bite people? That's how I got turned. Obviously." She grinned. "I mean, you were there."

"You've all been really lucky." The witch narrowed her gaze at Kerry. "You especially. A year alone with no pack and managing the change all by yourself... that's difficult. Deadly, even."

Vega reached out and grabbed his mate's hand and squeezed tight. Kerry leaned against him.

"What do you mean?" Stasia asked. "And why are you just telling us this now?"

The witch let out a sound of frustration. "Because I forget that you don't know this stuff! It's like why I don't mention the Earth revolves around the sun. I assume you already know because it's just fundamental knowledge and, frankly, it doesn't come up in conversation that often." She took a few deep breaths. "Sorry, as I was saying. Bitten shifters have a tendency to go feral or die. They don't turn right. Something about the change messes with brain chemistry—or maybe the structure of the brain itself, no one's really sure. But some bitten shifters become hyper aggressive and lose the ability to reason or communicate like people. Some of them fully complete the transformation—" she waved a hand, "I'm getting away from the important stuff. Anyway, it's risky to turn someone with a bite, and it means that you need to have a shifter under your control. If you turned mundane humans into shifters in some way you could control, then there's no trail back to a pack anywhere. Shifters have more innate magic than humans, and if you're careful, maybe you could do it over and over again. That's like seventy percent conjecture, but I've been puzzling over why Rosalie or anyone would go to the trouble of turning you all and then letting you go, but there it is. Either they didn't mean to let you go or turning you was basically proof of concept."

"So what does that mean for us?" Erin asked. "Can you do some magic to find Katrina? Maybe call in your coven for the big showdown? I know I'd like to get my claws into her." There was a hint of a growl in the back of Erin's throat.

Gibson approved. If his mate wanted five minutes alone in a locked room with the evil witch, he'd move heaven and earth to see it done.

But Vi didn't look confident. "Katrina was a member of my coven for her entire life. We're talking over forty years here. People like her. I don't think any of them would approve of what she's done, but to stand against her would take some convincing. And that's time we don't have."

"Why not?" Gibson asked.

"Because there was a hint of magic left in Erin, enough to track her. Katrina knows exactly where we are. And she's headed our way."

# CHAPTER TWENTY

THE ROOM ERUPTED into chaos after that, but Gibson wasn't having it. Erin watched with a not so secret thrill as he surged up off the chair and glared at everyone in the room that wasn't her.

"Silence!" It wasn't quite a roar—the man wasn't a lion, after all—but it made her shiver.

The room quieted, but the tension was thick.

"How do you know she's coming?" he asked Vi.

"Because she and whoever she's working with sank a ton of power into getting and keeping Erin. And I'm guessing that the pack has become too much of a hassle to deal with in these last few months. When you didn't know anything about the magical world, you weren't a threat. Now that you do..."

"We could blow all their plans up," Erin finished for her. Her shoulder ached with a phantom pain, and she was pretty sure she'd be scrubbing it raw the next time she jumped in the shower, but she trusted Vi. The magic was gone.

It was worse magic that was coming.

"I can't be certain, but it will take Katrina some time to gather her resources. They won't get here tonight. And, even if they did, my wards would keep them out. Not forever, but for awhile." Her back was straight, her mouth in a firm, determined line.

"You want to confront them," Gibson said.

Erin got out of the chair to stand beside him. "I'm guessing Katrina won't care too much about collateral damage. There's a lot of bystanders in Brooklyn."

Vi was nodding. "We know she's coming. You know this land. Three witches, even with one as powerful as Katrina, aren't a match for ten shifters and me, not when we've had time to prepare. If we do this now, you can finally have your answers. And it will be over."

Hope unfurled deep in Erin's chest. They could have some sort of normalcy, or as normal as it ever got for shapeshifters. What would that even look like?

She was desperate to find out.

Gibson turned to face the rest of the pack. "I can't make this call alone. This isn't what any of you signed up for. Any one of you can leave and I'll understand." That last bit went especially to Em and Kerry, Erin could tell. Em was a rock star when she wasn't busy being a shifter; she wasn't supposed to be fighting witches. And Kerry was the newest member of their pack, barely Vega's mate for two weeks. She was just getting over her own traumatic battles.

"I'm not leaving." Kerry was the first to speak. "You all saved my life, I won't run."

Em held her hand out in front of herself, palm up. Her brow furrowed as she concentrated. After a second, white light flashed and a circle of energy hovered above her hand. Neither Andre nor Stasia looked surprised, but the rest of the pack was staring at her wide eyed. "So you remember how I had to absorb all that magic when that ghost werewolf thing was chasing me? Yeah, the power never went away. I might be able to help on the magic end."

"I want magic werewolf powers!" Owen declared. His mate rolled her eyes, a small smile on her face.

It broke the remaining tension, and Erin let herself believe that they might actually win this thing if they played it right.

"So we fight," Gibson said, a mix of pride and resignation in his voice. "We need to get this place ready for battle. More importantly, I need all of you ready. Stuff can be replaced. I'd burn this entire house down before I let one of you fall. Make sure you sleep well."

"I can set up magical sentries on the roads into town," Vi offered. "They're not like the wards, and they won't do anything to stop Katrina or her allies, but we'll get some warning they're coming."

"Is it dangerous?" Gibson asked. "You told us not to leave the wards."

She shook her head. "I can do it at the edge of the wards and send the magic out. Not dangerous at all."

"Do it. Then do whatever it takes to recharge your magic. I have a feeling we're going to need it."

The group dispersed after that, most going to the bedrooms they'd claimed, with Owen sprinting for the downstairs bathroom on a promise he wouldn't use all the hot water with his shower.

Gibson held out a hand for Erin. She took it and followed him to his room.

It was simply decorated, with a photo of his family—that sister he'd mentioned and his niece, hanging beside a photo of him in his army uniform next to similarly dressed men that Erin didn't know. A TV took up most of one wall, and the walls themselves were a pale gray.

Erin sank onto Gibson's bed, her fingers curling into the dark blue comforter, soaking up the feel of the soft material as it scrunched under her fingers.

"This isn't the kind of thing I thought we'd have to deal with after getting out. I thought we left battle behind," she murmured. She wouldn't give Gibson up for anything, but she sometimes wished they had peace, or at least the kind of danger she understood.

Jericho's eyes softened and he stepped closer, his strong hands gently cradling her face, his touch igniting a fire beneath her skin. "I'd go into battle with you any day," he whispered, his breath warm on her lips.

His words sent shivers down her spine, her body aching for him. The world shrank until it was just the two of them, and the thoughts of battle were a distant threat, a problem for tomorrow.

Jericho leaned in, his lips capturing hers in a passionate kiss that made her blood sing.

God. Yes. She craved this, the taste of him on her tongue, the feel of his commanding lips pressed against her own as she succumbed to the wild hunger between them.

"Jericho," she gasped, the need to say his name, to acknowledge who they were when that door closed, too strong to ignore. His cock twitched against her thigh, and she heard the low growl rumbling in his chest.

It was a heady thing to be wanted by this man.

Jericho groaned, his mouth hot and hungry against her neck, his teeth teasing her skin hard enough to leave a mark. The love bite sent a shudder through her, a delicious mix of pain and intoxicating pleasure.

Then his lips were on hers again, drowning out her thoughts with the taste of his tongue, the heat of his body pressed against hers.

All that mattered was the searing heat between them. She tasted the primal hunger in his mouth, the raw power that hummed beneath his skin, and it ignited something wild within her, called to her own beast with a siren song she couldn't ignore.

He pressed her back against the soft comforter as they crashed back onto the bed.

"I missed you," Erin confessed, wrapping her

legs around his waist, clinging like some force might dare to part them again.

"It was too long," Jericho said, even if they both knew it had been only a day or so since they'd been alone, since they'd hidden themselves away from the world.

Her heart thudded against her chest, threatening to burst from the sheer intensity of sensation and the emotion that tried to overtake her.

He captured her lips in another fiery kiss. The warmth of his body pressed against hers, the feel of his strong hands roaming across her curves, made her dizzy with need.

Her fingers dug into the taut muscles of his back. She reveled in the connection they shared, the thing she'd been too scared to name before.

Mate.

Mate.

Mate.

"I love you." The confession burst out of her, the feeling too big to be contained.

He groaned and held her tighter, his lips buried at her neck, teeth barely scraping. "Love you too," he whispered against her skin, the words vibrating through her like a vow.

The sensation of Jericho's lips against her neck,

and of those words that went straight to her heart, sent shivers down her spine, and she couldn't do anything to stop the moan that escaped her throat.

"Shh," Jericho whispered against her skin.. "We don't want everyone hearing us, do we?"

It was a reminder of where they were, of the world waiting for them outside. And this was a private moment, something just for her and her mate. But keeping quiet was more challenging that it should have been, especially as Jericho's wicked lips tempted her.

"I need to taste more of you," he murmured, eyes dark with desire. His skilled hands made quick work of her top and bra, leaving her half-naked beneath him.

"I want to see you," she said, tugging at his shirt until he tore it over his head.

Erin ran her fingers through his chest hair, basking in the feel of the taut muscles underneath. Jericho's skin was warm, alive, and all there for her.

His lips trailed a blazing path down her body. He took a nipple into his mouth, sucking and nipping at the sensitive flesh while his other hand teased its twin.

Erin gasped, trying to keep quiet and knowing she was failing. Her fingers gripped the sheets as pleasure surged through her and her blood roared in her ears, drowning out everything but the fire Jericho ignited within her.

As Jericho's lips continued their journey down her body, he paused at the waistband of her jeans, and his fingers teased her until she shivered before his thumb flipped open the button. She couldn't help but let out a shaky breath as he slid the denim away from her hips, leaving her clad in nothing but her thin panties that she shimmied out of with possibly too much enthusiasm.

Her mate's eyes darkened with lust. He lowered his head once more, pressing a series of lingering kisses along the inside of her thighs, forcing Erin to bite her lip so hard she was afraid it might bleed. Her hands clutched at his broad shoulders, desperate to anchor herself amidst the storm of desire he stirred within her.

She arched her back, silently urging him on, and he finally relented, diving in to taste her slick heat.

He groaned against her, his tongue delving deep into her wet folds. He licked and kissed her with a hunger that was both intoxicating and overwhelming, and she writhed beneath him, gasps and moans too strong for her to even try to fight them.

"Let go for me," Jericho urged, his voice a low growl that rumbled against her.

With a strangled cry, she did, her entire body quaking with the force of it.

But it wasn't over, not that it ever could be between them. Even as she gasped, Jericho's lips found hers again, his tongue seeking entrance to her mouth, mingling with the taste of her own arousal.

Somehow, he'd managed to ditch his own pants, and Erin moaned as she felt his cock press against her. He groaned right back, his hands gripping her hips as if to anchor himself.

"I love you." She'd said it before, the words that had felt so impossible just days ago that now she couldn't keep in. The blue of Jericho's eyes was so intense it threatened to melt her from the inside, but there was a crushing tenderness to it, wrapping her up in his gaze until there could be nothing but safety in his arms.

"Say it again." His voice was low and urgent.

"I'm yours," she whispered, emotion so strong it threatened to clog the words in her throat. "Always yours."

The head of his cock nudged her entrance, teasing her with the promise of him. His fingers dug into her hips as he positioned himself, his gaze locked with hers, as if daring her to look away.

She was hot and wet, still trembling a bit from Jericho's lips on her, and she'd never needed him more than she did in this moment.

With a deep groan, Jericho thrust forward, burying himself within her slick heat. Erin cried out, unable to resist as her nails dug into his shoulders, and she let herself be swept away in a moment of pure bliss.

Then he moved and it was almost too much, his powerful body flexing and shifting above her as he began to thrust in earnest, his cock driving into her again and again until all she could do was hang on and feel.

Jericho's body trembled, his restraint cracking as he abandoned himself to the primal urges that drove him. Erin's fingers raked across his back, and she knew she'd left her own mark on him and felt seductive satisfaction.

"Mate," he growled, his eyes wild with a feral hunger. "Mate," he said again and again. "Mate, mate." It was a mantra that fueled his passion and bound them together.

"Mate," she gasped back, her voice barely more

than a whisper as she clung to him, her body arching up to meet his every powerful thrust.

She was so close, so desperate for more, and with a final thrust and the scrape of his teeth against her neck, she came, calling out his name far too loud for sense.

She didn't give a single damn.

Tomorrow was coming too soon, and war with it. Erin clutched Jericho close and let herself hope.

This would all be over one way or another. And then she'd have him to herself.

She wouldn't let any witch steal away her mate.

# CHAPTER TWENTY-ONE

Gibson left Erin sleeping in his bed, but the satisfaction of seeing her there, her face soft with sleep, ensconced in his sheets, followed him through the house and out the back door to the patio. The morning air was cool.

Autumn's hooks were well into Pennsylvania by now, and in another week or so his breath would be fogging in the chill.

He didn't let himself worry about what was coming. He refused to consider that he wouldn't walk away from this battle. And his mate?

He'd sell his soul to keep her safe.

But Erin was just as much soldier as he was, and there was no bundling her up and keeping her from the front lines. They'd run at danger side by side.

And they'd win.

He refused to consider any other option.

The woods were alive this morning, leaves swaying in the breeze, birds chirping, insects buzzing. There was no sign of a magical threat, no hint that by nightfall this place might be torn to shreds.

Vi hadn't said anything about her sensors, but Gibson didn't need magical powers to know that it wouldn't be long before they faced the enemy.

A small part of him was relieved. They'd been heading to this confrontation for years, even if he didn't know it. Ever since that night in the German woods when everything changed.

The door to the house slid open and Erin's scent enveloped him, warm and familiar and his. Gibson's inner wolf rumbled with satisfaction.

She handed him one of the two steaming coffee mugs in her hands and then leaned against his side. He looped his free arm around her shoulder.

Perfect.

If not for the impending battle.

"Has Vi said anything?" Erin asked quietly.

"Everyone's hiding from me this morning." With so many people in the house, even at this early hour, it was the only explanation for this private moment.

That brought a smile to his mate's lips. "Be honest, you love that we're all just a little afraid of you."

He turned fully to her, their gazes locking, and his wolf certainly in his eyes when he spoke. "I never want you to be afraid of me." He leaned down and kissed her. And though he wanted to devour her, to sink into the moment and let everything else slip away, he forced himself to pull back. It was why he'd left their bed this morning.

It still took more strength than he thought he possessed.

"There's nothing you could do... nothing you could ask and I wouldn't give you." They were feelings he'd done everything he could to push down for more than two and a half years, but after last night, there was no holding them back.

Erin's face was serious for a moment, and then she grinned widely. "That sounds like job security to me." They both laughed a little at that, then her face grew grim. "We need to figure that part out."

He kissed her forehead. "We will." Somehow.

It was good advice to not get involved with employees. Hell, it was an actual crime to fraternize in the army. But this thing with Erin was more important than any job. If that was the only obstacle left between them, Gibson would figure it out in no time.

He opened his mouth to say so, when someone cried out in front of the house. He and Erin dropped their mugs and sprinted inside, up the stairs, and out the front door, gathering a few pack members who saw them running and silently followed.

Em was beside the SUV she'd arrived in with Andre, brushing her hand against her legs and glaring at the road. The SUV was at the very end of the driveway, the back of it hanging out past the wooden fence that edged the ditch in the grass before the road.

Nothing was there.

Warning rumbled inside of him. This couldn't be good.

Em set her shoulders and stalked towards the end of the SUV, but she only made it as far as the back door before she stopped. She pressed her hand against the empty air and cursed. Then she leaned against it, her whole body pressing against nothing, as if there was an invisible wall there.

"Why does Em look like a mime?" Owen asked, joining the back of the group.

Em spun around. "I left a bag in the car. Now there's some magical wall that means I can't get it."

Vi muscled her way through to the front of the throng and joined Em, waving a hand around in front of her, brow furrowed.

"Katrina laid a ward on top of mine. That's... absurd." Her fingers sparked red with magic. "She has to be close. And she's blocking my notification wards." Vi's face was grim when she met his eyes. "We don't have much time."

Before Gibson could give an order, flame flickered at the edge of the property, sparking to encircle the house. But the flames weren't regular fire. They hovered above the grass, a green tint that spoke of the magic that powered them.

"That you?" he asked.

Vi shook her head. "It's a spell to eat through my wards." She looked towards the road and at the vacant lot across the street where some of the mud seemed to have been disturbed by a vehicle turning around. "They're right out there. Once the wards fall, they'll attack."

# CHAPTER TWENTY-TWO

THE ATTIC WAS HOT, stuffy in a way only attics could be. Erin pushed it out of her mind as she settled in next to the vent, the barrel of her rifle sticking through the slats. Sight wasn't good, not really. She'd prefer a window. But she was hidden up here.

Good.

She didn't want those damned witches to see her coming.

Her rifle was heavy in her hands, a familiar weight that she'd spent years training to carry. But this was an entirely different kind of war, one she'd never known she'd have to fight. And the responsibility nearly crushed her.

Her pack was out there. Her mate was out there. If she failed...

She wouldn't.

Outside, Em stood beside Vi, both of their hands glowing. Every move Vi made, Em made it a half-second later. Erin had zero clue what exactly it meant, but Vi had said it was vital.

Fire still ringed the house, Katrina's magic eating through Vi's wards. Erin wished a fire extinguisher would do something against it, but that was a false hope. The mundane was no threat to the magical.

She wasn't mundane anymore. She had claws and teeth, and she knew how to use them. And her handy rifle could stop a spell before the witch got a chance to fire it off.

Vi froze, Em following.

Behind them, Jericho and Rowe were silent sentinels, both giant wolves that would frighten anyone who spied them. Erin wanted to be down there with them. A part of her resented being relegated to the sniper position, even if it was because she was the best shot.

Was Jericho trying to protect her?

She pushed the thought aside. There was no room for doubts on the battlefield.

He was a storm inside her, the connection between them growing stronger and stronger with every kiss, every caress. It left a part of her feeling raw and exposed, but Erin wouldn't give it up for anything, and she refused to let some stupid witch end them before they truly began.

Erin's eyes were fixed on the magic gathering in Vi's and Em's hands. She couldn't yet see the enemy. They were obscured by the veil of magic eating into the wards.

This was more personal than any combat she'd faced before. It was one thing to march off on orders from Uncle Sam. This? This was her life, her family. And she'd do anything it took to keep them safe.

Some might have called it murder. But if she could have taken out Katrina with a knife in the dark, Erin would have reveled in it. Let it end before it began.

But it was too late for that now.

She glared down at the scene before her, ready for the wards to drop.

Let them come.

———

Battle sang in Rowe's blood. He prowled beside Gibson, his paws digging into the dirt deep enough to muddy his fur. That fur would be dirtied with blood before long.

Rowe craved it.

He wanted the wards to come down. He'd told his mate to do it, to let them fight it out with fur and claws. But his mate, his sexy, amazing, intelligent mate, wasn't as rash as him. And she was doing everything to protect them before that ward came down and chaos reigned.

Soon.

A growl gathered in the back of his throat, the need to charge singing loud and clear.

He could sense the magic all around him, both his mate's and that vile stuff just beyond the wards. He'd become more sensitive to it over the last few months, possibly from all the time spent around Vi.

Right now she commanded power as if she'd been born to it, and it made something deep inside of him practically purr, even if he was a wolf under his own skin.

Once this thing was over...

But there was no time for distraction on the battlefield, even if they were stuck in the interminable waiting process until the enemy took down the wards.

The fire around them flickered, almost normal,

almost real, but it stank of dark magic. Then it sputtered. Beside him, Gibson stilled. The magic flared in a single blast, and Rowe's ears popped.

The wards fell.

And standing at the very edge of the driveway was a woman he vaguely recognized who must have been Katrina. Beside her stood Stasia's brother, AR Selby. And the two of them were flanked by witches and shifters. More than the two that Vi had sensed in the spell on Erin.

The battle was on.

———

Stasia's fist curled tight, her own wolf prowling beneath her skin with the need to shift. She felt useless sitting in the living room, preparing the first aid kit and a makeshift surgery table made of sheet plastic on Gibson's nice carpet.

By night the whole thing might be smothered in blood.

Her pack's blood.

Her mate's blood.

She was their doctor, their healer, and this was where she needed to be, but it was its own battle not to rush outside and try to stem some of the bloodshed before it began. One more wolf on the side of her pack might mean the difference between life and death.

She hadn't been a fighter when she joined, when she was dragged into this world by an accidental bite and the desperation born of an accidental silver-based injury. But she could hold her own now. She and Owen had been training. Stasia refused to be helpless.

But she had to let the soldiers fight.

Her ears popped and something invisible dragged across her skin, and she knew with absolute certainty that the wards had fallen. Her breath puffed out in gasps, and she surveyed her surgery again.

Nothing to do but wait now.

Wait, and make sure she had at least two exit paths. If something happened to the house, she needed a way out. She had three: the front door, the downstairs door, and the window that looked out over the front yard. That last one would be a bit of a drop, but Stasia was tough, and if it was between a ten foot leap and dying, the choice was simple.

She was supposed to stay away from the windows, to make herself less of a target and keep attention off the house. But Stasia couldn't resist creeping close and peeking out. The curtain obscured most of the view, hiding her from sight, but if she angled herself just right, she could peek through a crack and see what was happening.

*You goddamn bastard.*

Her eyes snagged on her eldest brother, AR, and she scowled.

He'd been mixed up in this from the very beginning, had set her on a path to meet Owen just to have a closer connection to the men and women he'd had transformed into shifters for some nefarious purpose.

Had he warned Stasia about it? Of course not.

And now he was here for... what?

Stasia knew her brother was heartless, was the exact kind of cold, unfeeling man that her father had raised him to be. She'd run from that family as far and as fast as she could, and even still she was sometimes burned by the chill of Selby love.

Had he really come here to kill them?

AR looked away from the witch at his side and right towards the house, as if he had some special sense, some way to see her. It was a knife to Stasia's gut.

AR looked bad. Even from a distance she could see the bags under his eyes. His suit was looser than it should have been and wrinkled, as if he'd been in it for days.

He was supposed to be in Europe, far away from this battle and the magic swirling around them.

Stasia was supposed to stay put.

But she had to move, had to talk to him, even if it was foolish. Maybe she could find a way to end this whole thing, get AR to call it off.

Katrina shot a bolt of magic towards Gibson and chaos erupted.

Stasia moved. By the time she was out the front door, the entire place was so distracted no one noticed. AR had a knife clutched in one hand and something else she couldn't quite see in the other, but his face was completely pale and he was shaking.

He didn't want to be here. Whatever was going on, he'd lost control of the situation. At the end of the day, he was still just a human in a world of magic. Money wasn't the only power here.

While two shifters lunged at Rowe, Katrina engaged Gibson and Vi. Another witch was throwing shots of magic out, but they seemed more like a distraction than anything else.

A bullet whizzed by overhead, but the air above

the battle thickened, making it appear the bullet was traveling through some kind of jelly.

The extra witch looked up and smiled, pointing towards the attic where Erin was hiding with her rifle. The witch hurled a glowing orb of yellow magic right at the house and tore a hole through the vent where Erin was supposed to be.

Stasia didn't let herself consider the possibilities. Erin was quick, and she'd already survived so much. A tiny bolt of magic was nothing. Even if flames, actual fire now, were licking at the siding of the house.

AR spotted her and lunged her way, dropping the knife. Stasia met him head on, but not to fight.

"What the hell?" she demanded. It felt like a yell, but the battle was quieter than she expected, magic only a whisper interspersed with growls and howls and the occasional scream of pain.

"Where's Em?" he shot right back, looking around as if their other sister wasn't standing right next to Vi, her own hands glowing with magic. "Come on, I can get us out of here. Kat's distracted."

Stasia blinked at him, her brain stuttering. "What the hell are you talking about? You're the one attacking us!" She wanted to scream, but she kept her voice quiet. No one had noticed them talking yet, and she didn't want to attract attention, not while battle raged around them.

"You're my sister, of course I want to get you out of this. Em, too. Let Kat deal with the others. We'll get away clean and figure out how to fix the two of you." He reached out to grab her.

Stasia staggered back. "There's nothing to fix. Why are you doing this?" As she asked, she realized the need to know the answer was the reason she'd come out.

"I came to rescue you." He said it like it was obvious.

This was hopeless. And Stasia had been a fool. A reckless fool. This wasn't where she belonged, and AR had been beyond saving for a long time. She shook her head and backed up a step.

AR reached into his pocket, but before he could do anything else, Stasia heard a growl and then felt the searing heat as a wolf pounced and tackled her to the ground.

# CHAPTER TWENTY-THREE

OWEN FELT the tug on the bond that connected him and Stasia and sprinted, his four paws carrying him faster than he'd ever run, just in time to see an enemy wolf crash into her. He quickly noted AR Selby standing there, glaring and frozen.

The useless bastard wasn't doing a thing to help his sister.

And if Owen wasn't so occupied with protecting his mate, he would have done something about it. Instead, he dug his teeth into the enemy wolf and tore it off of Stasia, putting himself between his mate and harm.

Stasia was supposed to be inside. She was supposed to be as safe as anyone could be right now.

But maybe the fire quietly smoldering along the side of the house had sent her running.

Or maybe it was her sorry excuse of a brother.

All that was pushed aside as Owen let his beast run free, his teeth stained with blood and thirsty for more. No one hurt his mate, his pack, not without paying for it.

There was a sick kind of satisfaction running through his veins. One year ago he'd met his mate, one year ago his life had become whole in a way he'd never known to dream of. But lingering under all of that had been questions.

Now, they had their answers. Now it was almost over.

Owen pounced again, but the wolf was wily and twisted out of his grip. It looked over his shoulder so quick that Owen almost missed it, and then it was off running. Owen was tempted to follow. Almost.

But not while Stasia was down.

Owen bounded over to her, still wearing his fur. He might have shifted, but she was already sitting, brushing dirt off her arm. Her shirt was ripped, but he didn't see any blood. She was okay.

As long as she was okay, Owen was fine.

He looked over to AR, but Stasia's brother was gone.

---

Andre's soul strained in his fur. His mate was out of sight, on the front line and facing off a force they couldn't fight without her. It took all of his discipline not to bound around the house and face her enemies.

Gibson was there. So was Rowe. And if anyone would keep Em safe, it was them.

He and Hunter had to guard their flank, to make sure that no one came in through the woods and caught them by surprise. It was frustrating work. There were miles of forest and he should have been able to tell by scent alone if they were in danger.

But magic didn't give a single damn about his senses.

He growled, and Hunter huffed out a quizzical sound. Neither of them could speak in their wolf forms, but what did that matter? It all meant the same thing.

The threat didn't come from the woods.

A bolt of magic zinged his way, coming from the field beside the house. The open field, where Andre could see for miles. Except the air of that field shimmered in a way it shouldn't, and one breath later it split in two and vomited a witch and two wolves who ran straight at him and Hunter.

The first wolf hit him as magic shot overhead. Hunter yelped, but Andre had to block it out. She could handle herself in a fight, she had to.

The wolf kept coming, even when Andre's teeth gouged a terrible hole in its side. It attacked like it couldn't feel pain, like there was nothing it wanted more than to destroy Andre and everything he held dear.

Andre fought back, pushing everything else aside, even concern for Em. If he didn't take these wolves out now, they'd get to her. This was the only way he could help.

The plan might have worked... if it weren't for the witch.

A bolt of magic caught Andre on his side and he yelped, pain searing through him faster than he could think. The wolf crashed into him, digging its teeth into the fur near his shoulder, just barely missing his neck.

It was pure luck, but Andre couldn't use it. It couldn't turn the tide in his favor, not when every nerve was on fire with the remnants of that spell.

He'd fought magic once before, and somehow this was worse. Then, he'd been squaring off against an enemy he couldn't see, but it hadn't been trained on him. Now, he was the target, and the magic didn't want to let go.

Another bolt hit him and he whimpered, but for some reason the wolf had stopped attacking. Andre didn't have time to wonder why. He rolled to his side, doing his best to protect his belly before the wolf could come back. But he was hurt and hurting, too distracted by the magic to be any good to Hunter or anyone else.

The witch grinned an evil smirk and raised his hand, dark purple magic glowing its sinister light.

But before he could shoot that fatal shot at Andre, a wolf barreled into the witch and sent him sprawling.

———

Kerry wasn't a fighter. Some days she still had to wrap her mind around the fact that she was a freaking shapeshifter.

But that didn't matter as she launched herself at the witch with the freaky glowing hands and snapped, using claws and teeth until the witch stopped moving and the magic faded.

Andre, in wolf form, writhed on the ground

nearby, and Bryan approached carefully, nudging at him with his snout.

Once the witch stopped moving, Andre rebounded, jumping to his paws as if nothing could stop him and growling in Hunter's direction.

The wolf was facing off with two others. They had her cornered against the side of the house and Kerry could practically smell the bloodlust in the air.

Not today. They weren't losing anyone in this fight. She refused.

With the odds shifted, the enemy wolves didn't stand a chance.

Kerry might have nightmares about it later, about the way blood sprayed her fur, the tang of it sharp on her tongue.

Those nightmares could swirl around with all the other ones. It didn't matter, not so long as she helped her pack survive this fight.

She exchanged a look with Hunter, but that woman was in her element, the battle shining in her wolfish eyes as she tore into one of her opponents and let out a howl of victory as the enemy wolf whimpered and fell.

Kerry had the pack's backs as Bryan and the others finished the wolves off. The violence of it turned Kerry's stomach, but she wouldn't retreat.

She'd been dragged into this world against her will, but she was here now and she wanted to stay. She had a mate, a pack, and she couldn't ask for more.

Well, perhaps she could ask for this battle to end, but that would happen. One way or another.

The enemy wolves were down. The witch was taken care of.

Kerry brushed up against Bryan, letting herself feel a moment of triumph.

It lasted only long enough for a scream from the other side of the house to rent the air.

Kerry went running.

———

Smoke tickled her nose, but that wasn't enough to get Erin to abandon her position. The fire was eating into the siding of the house, but with every inch it covered, it seemed closer to dying, sputtering out into property damage and the memory of flame.

Wolves fought wolves while witches sat back as best they could and engaged from a safe distance. Erin had tried more than once to shoot Katrina Stevens square in the forehead, but there was some magical force preventing it. Her bullets flew true, but then seemed to encounter an invisible wall of magic that made it appear they were flying through ballistics gel until they dropped harmlessly to the ground.

Erin wasn't supposed to be able to *see* the bullets after she shot them.

She was wasted where she was, and that grew more obvious by the moment. This was a magical fight, there was no place for guns.

But Erin's training, her discipline, ran deep. It kept her in place long past when she wanted to move and was almost strong enough to keep her there when a bolt of magic sent Gibson flying through the air and tumbling into a bush in front of the house.

Fuck it. She was gone.

Erin moved so fast she might have actually tele-ported. At least that's what it felt like. One moment she was in the attic, the next she knew she was on the field, grabbing an enemy wolf with her bare *human* hands and fighting like she could win.

Her instincts screamed at her to find Gibson, to find her mate, but it was chaos, and she couldn't see him through the haze of magic all around her.

He had to be okay. She'd know if he wasn't.

That was a refrain Erin let play through her head as she met every enemy head on, finally remembering to pull out her knife and even the playing field between herself and the wolves.

A few wolves and one witch lay unmoving on the ground, but the rest of the wolves attacked with a ferocity Erin had never seen before. This was more than battle rage. And when she spotted a witch aim a blast of power at an enemy wolf, she started to understand.

Those wolves might hurt, but the witches were healing them, or, if not that, doing something to keep them upright. They wouldn't go down until there was no getting up again.

Erin headed for the witches.

No one noticed her, and she swept past where Owen was tearing into a wolf without either of them glancing her way. For half a second she wondered if this was some sort of magic, if she was being summoned, but she suspected it was just luck. Katrina and her people fought too chaotically to be called an army, and they had no training. It was why her wolves and witches lay dead while the smaller force of Erin and her pack held them off.

For now. An untrained force, especially a big one, was bound to get lucky.

A feminine scream cut through Erin's march and she paused, turning her head.

Stasia.

Fuck.

The pack doctor was fending off a wolf while a witch pelted her with magic. Stasia could hold her own in a fight, Erin knew, Owen had been training her for months. But two on one where one of those enemies had magic? Stasia didn't stand a chance.

Erin changed her trajectory, coming up behind the witch and ending her with one swipe of a knife.

Somehow it distracted the wolf, and Stasia got in her shot. The wolf went down.

It didn't get back up.

Stasia wiped her forehead with the back of her palm, smudging some blood along her face. It didn't seem to bother her. "You're not supposed to be down here," she said.

Erin grinned. "I couldn't let you have all the fun without me."

Anything else they might have said was cut short by another wolf charging at them. Erin regretted not shifting to her other form, but it would take too long now and leave her vulnerable during the shift. She let the regret fall away, it had no place here.

But before the wolf could hit them, it clattered to a halt, skidding on the mud and snarling. Erin didn't dare take her eyes off of it, but she also didn't get any closer. If some sort of magic was interfering with the wolf, she didn't want to get caught up in it.

"Go fight someone else," a male voice said. Erin didn't recognize it, which meant it wasn't one of her pack members.

She squared up, ready for a fight.

Stasia stumbled forward and came to a halt. "AR." It was a choked off word filled with the kind of emotion that didn't belong in the middle of this kind of fight.

So this was Stasia's brother. She expected someone more impressive, to be honest. But AR had never done anything for himself. He had waited out his old life and was still waiting to inherit his father's company. And rather than turn himself into a shifter, he had put his sister in the path of the pack and watched everything play out without warning.

Erin bared her teeth. This piece of shit was about to get what was coming to him.

AR glanced back over his shoulder. "Stasia, come on. You don't have to be here."

"I could say the same for you." There was more emotion in the doctor's voice than Erin had ever heard before. Stasia was normally even toned, and sometimes harsh. She saved the softer emotions for her mate, Erin assumed. "Why are you doing this? What's going on?"

Erin's eyes flicked to the magic device he had in his hand. It could control shifters. He had sent that other wolf running. But he wasn't using it on them. Not yet. Erin shifted on her feet and AR looked over at her, his hand twitching and aiming the magical device at her. If it was anything like the one she had encountered on the ship, she didn't want him using it. There was little she could do to fight it.

"Do you have any idea what kind of power these people are offering?" AR scoffed. "Do you know what I could do with it?"

"You already have a ton of power," Stasia spat out. "I know the size of your trust fund. Of what you're about to inherit. Is this all because our father hasn't died? You're one of the richest people in the country. Why care about magic?"

AR's scowl deepened. "You don't understand. You had everything given to you."

Stasia laughed. "Me? Right. You never..." Stasia let out a deep breath. "Just leave this place, AR. Let it go. You don't have to do this."

Unfortunately, that had the opposite effect on Stasia's brother. He raised his hand and the device in it began to glow.

"Run, Stasia," Erin muttered, hoping that AR couldn't hear her. "I'll cover you."

Stasia didn't run. "Stay still," AR commanded, and the force of it gripped Erin tight. She couldn't even clench her fingers. She tried to fight it, but no matter how much she strained, her body wouldn't let her.

AR looked directly at her for a second, as if he couldn't decide what to do with her. If he told her to die, would she? Did that device have so much power? She needed to destroy it. She didn't want anything like that existing in the world.

She was so focused on AR that she didn't hear the second person approach until they were already within striking distance. The woman looked a bit older than Erin, and wore a tight black tactical outfit. Her nails were painted black and bright red energy circled around them.

"You caught two, human." She gave AR a wolfish smile. "Well done. Finish them, and let's move on."

The light surrounding the witch's fingers flickered for a moment before disappearing like a candle that had been blown out.

Erin might have said something about that, but AR's device was still holding her tight and there was no way she could say a word.

"It's fine," said AR, his tone with the kind of finality that would make a person in a board room flinch. "Go deal with something else."

The witch gave him a disbelieving look. "You aren't my boss. Finish them."

AR gulped, but he raised the device and aimed it at Erin. She didn't let herself think of regrets, and she definitely didn't let herself think about Gibson. But AR hesitated.

The witch let out a curse and then raised her own hand toward Erin, the red light flickering back to life for a moment. She punched her hand out toward Erin, as if she was trying to send a bolt of energy through the short space between them. But nothing happened.

Then, faster than Erin realized what was happening, the wicked witch reared back and clamped her hand onto AR's neck. Her hand flared bright red, and AR screamed, dropping the device.

The hold on Erin evaporated, and she launched herself at the witch, digging her knife into the woman before she had a chance to realize Erin and Stasia were free. But even as the witch fell, AR screamed.

# CHAPTER TWENTY-FOUR

KATRINA WOULD LET every single one of her witches and wolves die before anyone got close to her, Gibson realized. He'd been cut in several places, but he wasn't bleeding profusely. His muscles ached, and it was only the fact that he had four feet instead of two at the moment that kept him standing.

That, and the need to protect his pack, his mate.

Vi shot bolts of magic at anyone who got close to her, but Em's own magic had flickered out half an hour ago. She had run for cover but came back within minutes, shifted into her wolf form, and ready to do battle.

Gibson couldn't let harm come to any of these people. They were all his, and he took that responsibility to heart. An enemy wolf lunged at him, and

Gibson buried his teeth into the creature's fur and shook with all his might, sending the creature flying. This wasn't how he was trained for battle. This wasn't what he was meant to do, or perhaps it was. Perhaps fate had a way of finding the people it needed and putting them in these kinds of situations to test who they truly were.

They needed to get to Katrina.

Gibson charged, but he was intercepted by another witch who went down under his claws. Rowe ran right after him, trying to use the distraction to his advantage, but Katrina nearly incinerated him with a nasty bolt of magic.

Their numbers were thinning. As far as Gibson knew, he had not lost any of his wolves, but Katrina's forces lay still on the ground. Not enough of them. The wolves fought with an unholy energy, powering through injuries that would have taken any normal beast down. Was it magic? He couldn't be sure. But he knew that showing mercy wasn't working. When he tried to leave a wolf injured rather than dead, the wolf sprang back to its feet and attacked him as if mercy was an insult.

Gibson kept fighting.

He hadn't heard a shot from overhead in a while

and was trying not to think about the fire ripping through his attic. Erin was okay. He had seen the way the magic ate up her bullets. And though he wanted her in the safest position, his selfish heart doing what it could to keep her safe, his soldier of a mate would not stay back where she was useless. He had a feeling she had waded into the fight. And he needed this fight to end before Katrina set her eyes on Erin.

Gibson fell back behind Vi to find Rowe already there, waiting for him. Hunter was beside them, her smaller wolf form free of any injury. She barked out a greeting, and Gibson bared his teeth, which might have been a smile in another form but edged onto a threat in this one.

"Give me two seconds," Vi muttered back to them. "She's got a real asshole of a ward up. When I say run, run at her."

The scent of magic tickled Gibson's nose, and he wondered if anyone could be allergic to it. It made him want to sneeze. He didn't have any more time to think about it as Vi gave the word, and the three wolves charged.

Katrina watched them come, as if she didn't think that they could get anywhere near her. *What have I done?* He trusted the witch with his life, with his pack. If she said they should charge, there must be a way to take Katrina out.

Katrina's gaze met his, and she smiled cruelly, raising a hand and pointing it straight at him. Gibson didn't see the blast of magic, but it sent him flying back, crashing into the ground with a yelp of pain as agony shot through him.

---

Screw human form, Erin had taken the opportunity to shift into her wolf form and bounded towards the center of the action, where her pack was trying to take out the evil witch responsible for all of this bullshit and heartache.

She was almost there when she saw Gibson fly through the air and land with a yelp of pain. Every instinct in her demanded that she go to her mate, that she check on him and make sure he was okay. But Erin forced herself to stay on her path. She could do nothing for him in this form, nothing but fight and end this.

Rowe and Hunter had engaged Katrina and were dancing between her bolts of magic. She cursed at them, both in the traditional way and magically.

She didn't see Erin come up behind her. She

didn't feel it when Erin lunged and tackled her to the ground.

Erin had the perfect shot to dig her teeth into Katrina's throat and end this once and for all. Instead, she swiped her claws down the witch's side and felt grim satisfaction as the woman screamed. Katrina had hurt her mate, Erin was going to hurt her right back.

Her mistake became evident nearly as soon as she began. Katrina reached out, heedless of the blood running down her side, and dug a hand into Erin's fur. She muttered some kind of dark spell that Erin couldn't understand. Erin tried to pull away. It should have been easy. She was stronger than Katrina in this form, and the woman did not have a strong grip. But Erin was frozen as Katrina's fingers tightened on her fur and then ripped away, taking something from deep inside of her with them.

Erin yelped, but it didn't come out of her wolfish throat.

She didn't even feel the change take her. One second she was a wolf, the next she was a naked human woman kneeling at Katrina's feet.

"What—" Erin looked at Katrina, eyes wide, but she came to her senses in less than a second and scrambled out of the way before Katrina could do something with whatever magic she had just stolen from Erin.

Erin scampered away, her body frozen with the sudden chill of nakedness, and her chest utterly empty. It felt as if her very soul had been ripped out from the center of her, and she couldn't stop herself from bending over and emptying her stomach, the vomit vile in her mouth.

She felt, and then heard, Katrina scream, and finally looked over to see Gibson looming over the witch, his claws buried in her chest. Katrina's hand twitched, dark magic hovering over it, and Erin tried to cry out a warning, but her voice was completely gone, her throat hoarse with whatever evil Katrina had wrought.

But the warning was unnecessary. Gibson didn't waste time trying to make her suffer. He dug his teeth into her throat, and then it was done. Erin sagged in relief, some of the darkness holding onto her snapping as she realized whatever spell Katrina had done to her had let go completely.

Vi was the first one to get to her, and she slipped out of her jacket and offered it to Erin. Erin pulled it on, thankful for the covering.

She looked around the battlefield that was Gibson's house. There should still have been wolves and witches all around them; they hadn't killed everyone. But even the few they had managed to take out were gone. There was no one except for Katrina's body.

And then Erin heard Stasia's sob.

She was a bit unsteady on her feet as she made her way back to where Stasia was hovering over AR, whose labored breathing suggested he wasn't long for this world. Vi was right behind Erin, the rest of the pack, all of them in their wolf forms, converging behind her.

"Is there anything you can do?" Stasia asked in broken gasps. "I don't see any injuries. I can't fix it."

Vi knelt down and placed her hand over the angry red mark at AR's neck. "His vital magic was drained." He gasped and went taut, and Vi flinched. "I'm sorry, that's all I can do. You have enough time to say goodbye." She took a step back.

Stasia's face hardened, and she stared down at her brother. He opened his eyes, but they didn't seem to focus on anything.

"Why, AR?" she asked, her voice hard this time.

"Too good of an opportunity. So much power. The witch told me I could have it all. We could steal it from the shifters, and no one would know. It would come back. Over and over again. Where is she? What happened?" He gasped again and tried to sit up, but he didn't have the energy. A few more labored breaths were all he managed.

Em came up beside Stasia and leaned into her sister. They both sat vigil while the last of his energy drained from him, and he died.

Gibson came up to Erin's side, and she let her hand rest in his fur. The two of them turned away from the sisters. The rest of the pack, except for the sisters' mates, turned away as well, giving them privacy. They might have won, but the sisters needed this moment to deal with their loss.

# CHAPTER TWENTY-FIVE

In the week that followed, Gibson couldn't quite believe that it was over. He was thankful for Vi's magic when it came to getting rid of Katrina and the evidence of the battle, and he decided not to ask too many questions when she seemed very competent at hiding evidence. Perhaps it was for the best. Stasia and Em were both subdued as they thought up the story they would need to feed their family about AR's disappearance. Eventually, Vi suggested that they place his body on a hiking trail to make it appear that an accident had befallen him.

He didn't suffer from any external wounds. She explained that a witch had sucked the life force out of him, and to any coroner, it might appear like dehydration or exhaustion.

Em was reluctant at first, but Stasia agreed, and Gibson had Vi and Rowe take care of it.

The rest of the pack had not so subtly left him and Erin to their own devices as soon as they fixed the superficial damage to his house. Luckily, the fire had been the worst of it, and it hadn't been as bad as he feared in the midst of the battle.

He would have to get an inspector out sometime to make sure that there were no hidden secrets that would send the house collapsing into a pile of wood and rubble, but it seemed sturdy enough for now.

He made love to his mate with the ferocity of a man who knew he had almost lost her. And Erin returned the feelings to him tenfold.

But there was something wrong. Something she was holding back.

At first, he thought it was just the battle fatigue setting in. Some people recovered from fighting like it was nothing, others needed time. And they had time now. If AR's dying words were to be believed, Katrina and AR and whoever else they had been working with were gone.

Yes, not all of the witches were dead, but they had cut off the head of the beast. If the witches and wolves who had been working for Katrina were smart, they would scatter to the winds and never be heard from again.

At least for now, Gibson let himself believe that was the case.

He found Erin sitting on a bench on the patio out back, staring into the empty fire pit. Her face was haggard, the bags under her eyes making it look like she hadn't slept in a week, something he knew was utterly false as he had slept beside her every night.

He sat down next to her, and she leaned against him, her head resting on his shoulder as he slung his arm around her and held her close.

"Do you want to go for a run?" he asked. They hadn't done that since before the battle, and Gibson's wolf was anxious under his skin.

Erin stiffened. And then a sob tore out of her. "I can't!" She crumpled in her seat.

"Why not?" His own heart broke at the pain in her voice, but he wouldn't let go. Not of her, not ever.

"I can't shift," Erin confessed. "I've tried it every day since the fight, since Katrina did something to me. It was like she pulled my wolf out of me, and I can't even feel it anymore. There's nothing there. Nothing at all."

Gibson wasn't surprised. He should have been. It

should have been the kind of thing that tore through him, the shock that would send him rocking back on his feet. But as he thought back over the last week and the things that Erin didn't say, it made its own kind of sense.

He held on tight, not knowing how to respond. "I love you," he finally said. That would always be true.

Erin wrapped her own arms around his midsection and held on tightly, tears beginning to soak his shirt.

"I talked to Vi," she said. "She said she'd never heard of something like that. That it shouldn't be possible. She said she thought my wolf should come back to me in a few days or weeks. But it's not. It's gone. I can tell."

"We can ask another witch," Gibson offered, though there wasn't one he trusted more than Vi.

Erin pulled back a little so that she could meet his eyes. Hers were firm with determination. "I want you to bite me. I want you to turn me back into a wolf."

For some reason, everything in Gibson revolted at that. Not because he wanted Erin to remain human. He wanted the joy of running through the forest with his mate, of knowing that she had that other form, and that strength inside of her. There was nothing he would deny her.

But he remembered the pain that Stasia had gone through when she was bitten. He knew that Em had almost died from her bite. And Vi had implied that it could be dangerous, and that they had been lucky.

"One more week," he said. "Let's give it another week to see if your wolf comes back. Then we talk to Vi."

And he would pray every day that Erin's wolf returned.

———

Erin's wolf didn't return in the next week, nor in the three days after that. Erin was full of restless energy and desperate for Gibson to get over whatever was holding him back and just freaking bite her already.

They had briefly gone back to the city and back to his apartment. Erin realized it was the first time she had been to Jericho's place in the city. It was exactly what she expected: refined, a bit boring on the decoration, but decently sized, and with a bed comfortable enough and more than big enough for the two of them. That was all that mattered.

But they were back at the farmhouse again, and this time Vi was there with them. They sat on the back patio, Erin's hand in Jericho's, and spoke with the witch.

"It's dangerous," said Vi. "I don't know if there is something about your magical transformations that made it so that Stasia and Em transformed all right, but there's a risk."

"I want to be a wolf again," Erin said, trying to ignore whatever that risk might be.

"What risk?" Gibson asked.

Vi pursed her lips and took a deep breath, her shoulders set in a straight line. "Death, to start off with. The longer the transformation takes, the more risk there is. We can mitigate that. I can speed along the transformation magically, like I did with Em. It will be painful, but fast. But there's another risk. Shifters can go feral. Something about the change causes them to lose themselves. They become beings set on causing as much pain, destruction, and damage as possible."

"So I would go crazy? Like rabid or something?" It gave Erin a second of pause. Would it really be worth the risk?

Vi shook her head. "It's not that simple. Feral wolves are dangerous because they are hard to spot.

They're capable of conversation, of hiding some of their violence. They're smart, cunning, and absolutely ruthless. It's like something in their brain breaks during the change. I've heard of wolves going feral after they've changed, and sometimes it occurs in born shifters, but it most likely happens immediately after the transformation."

"Why haven't you told us about this before?" Gibson demanded. He squeezed Erin's hand tighter, as if that would be enough to keep her safe.

Vi leveled a look at him. "We've been a bit busy. And what was the point? It's not like you've been going around and changing a ton of people into wolves."

"I still want it." Maybe Erin was being rash, maybe she could learn to live with being a normal human again, but she knew what it felt like to transform, and she wanted it back. "What are the odds?"

"I don't know. There's no way to know. Maybe using magic makes it less likely. I haven't heard of that many feral wolves. A few dozen out of a hundred thousand. Maybe." She didn't look certain of her numbers.

"There are hundreds of thousands of shifters?" Gibson asked, eyes wide.

Vi nodded. "Oh, at least. There are seven billion

people on the planet. A good number of wolves out there. And tigers. Lions. Coyotes. Lots of animals."

"A couple dozen out of hundreds of thousands aren't bad odds," Erin said. She was sure she did things that were more risky than that on a weekly basis. She looked to Gibson. "Will you do it, Jericho?" It was a low blow, to use his name like that.

He squeezed her hand and let out a breath full of fear and hope. "Yes." He turned to Vi. "When?"

"I'm ready now," the witch replied. "You just need to shift forms. I'll give you two a minute." She headed back inside.

Gibson cupped Erin's cheek and leaned forward, brushing a kiss against her lips. "You know I don't care whether or not you're a wolf," he told her.

Erin wrapped her fingers around his biceps and kissed him right back. "But I care."

"I want to get married." It burst out of Gibson like a dam breaking.

"What?" Erin jolted.

Jericho grinned at her. "I want to marry you. What do you say?"

"Is this really the time for a proposal?" Laughter threatened to bubble up out of Erin, pure joy that the man in front of her was hers.

"Considering the discussion we just had with Vi,

yes, this is exactly the time." Jericho was grinning down at her, as if he knew that her hesitation, her resistance, had nothing to do with him and everything to do with surprise.

"Fine," Erin said, still grinning. "You turn me back into a wolf, and I'll marry you."

"You're on." He pulled his shirt off, and Erin grinned, watching as he stripped down to nothing and enjoying the view.

She glanced away as he shifted to give him that little bit of privacy, and a moment later, he was in his magnificent wolf form before her.

Vi joined them shortly after that. She summoned magic to her hands and nodded at Gibson. Erin held out her forearm right in front of his mouth.

He reached forward and clamped down hard enough that Erin couldn't suppress the gasp of pain.

But that was nothing compared to the torrent of agony that rushed through her the second Vi's magic touched her and everything went black.

Agony ripped through her as she sank into the darkness, consciousness gone but fear and pain still her fast friends. She felt herself flung apart and squashed back together, everything rearranged but nothing quite right.

When Erin came to, she felt short. Short, and

hunched over. On four legs. With fur. And claws. And teeth.

She was a wolf again.

Erin tilted her head back and howled in joy and relief, the emotions sharp and simple in her animal form. Her mate joined her. And then they took off running, heading into the woods behind the farm and running to chase the sunset.

# CHAPTER TWENTY-SIX

Erin lay back on the bed, her short white dress crumpled underneath her legs, and held her hand up above her face, admiring the white gold band on her finger. The bed dipped beside her as Jericho plopped down next to her, head propped on one hand, his smile broad.

"We really just did that," she said, curling her hand to a fist and lowering it.

He laughed, the sound encircling her with warmth. "Try not to sound so shocked."

Erin reached for his hand and found the matching ring on his finger. She ran her thumb over it, the metal warm under her touch.

Rowdy laughter echoed through the window, the rest of the pack still outside and eating their way through a mountain of food and alcohol. There had been a lascivious grin or two when she and her mate decided to sneak inside, but it sounded like the fun was easily going on without them.

"I'm sorry your sister couldn't make it." A sudden storm had delayed her flight, and Erin's own family couldn't get the time off work. That's what happened when you planned a wedding in less than a month.

"I think she's still getting over the fact that I told her about the wedding in the same text I told her we were together." Jericho laced their fingers together.

Erin squeezed, heart too happy for the slightest bit of regret. Was it fast? Maybe. But she and Jericho had been dancing around one another for years, and they had the hand of fate guiding them. She didn't have a doubt about this man. Why wait?

"We'll meet her tomorrow," Erin offered. "And maybe it's better if we don't inflict the entire pack on her at once."

Her mate reached over and cupped her cheek. "Do you really want to talk about my sister right now?" Jericho captured her lips in a hungry kiss and Erin let all thoughts about tomorrow drift away as she sank into it.

She couldn't get enough of him, never would.

The fire between them burned too bright for her to ignore, not that she wanted to, not now that she could revel in this connection.

The hard length of his cock pressed against her through their clothes, but Erin let herself enjoy the kiss without much urgency. They had all night. All week.

Forever.

She let out a small gasp and her lips curved under his as his arms wrapped around her, pulling her close. His body was heavy beside her, his scent swirling around and going to her head.

She let her fingers trail down his body and felt a surge of feminine power as he growled deep in his throat as she teased him over his trousers. She ached for him, and the hardness under her palm was more than enough proof to show he needed her just as much.

As if she didn't receive that proof every day.

She'd never particularly cared about marriage before, assuming it would happen if it happened, but now with her husband—husband!—right here with her, she didn't know how she'd waited so long.

"Please," she gasped out, not exactly sure what she was asking for. Her hand curled around his thick length and stroked through fabric until Jericho thrust against her, powerless to stop.

"I need you," he growled, hips lips trailing a searing path along her jawline and down her throat. Her pulse thundered, blood rushing in her ears and making her just a bit light headed. Still she wanted more.

But her mate was a man of discipline, no matter his need, and though she wanted him to flip her over and fucking take her, he let gentle kisses trail down her body, slowly undoing the zipper of her dress until she could ease her way out of it while barely needing to part from him.

He groaned when he saw the delicate lace panties she wore.

Her smile turned into an impish grin and she delighted in the ways his eyes darkened as he took her in. Her whole body was tight with anticipation, and she ran a finger down the center of her chest, letting it drag under one of her breasts and the lacy confection of her bra that was mostly decoration rather than support.

"Do you want me to tear it off?" From the glint in his eye, he might be planning to do it with his teeth.

He tugged and it gave way easily, leaving Erin

bare with only the tiny scrap of her panties that Jericho dealt with like they were nothing. He sucked in a deep breath once she was completely revealed to him and Erin arched up, stretching her arms and making a display, her body tightening even more, her core hot and aching for him.

But Erin wasn't content to just lie there, not when her mate was looking at her like she was a cake he couldn't wait to feast on.

Two could play at that game.

With a sudden burst of energy, she sat up and dragged Jericho down, her hand going to the clasp of his pants and tugging them down. She wasn't going to be the only naked person in this room.

His freed cock was hard and throbbing as his pants crumpled to the floor, and Erin took it in her hand, a wicked grin in her eyes as she met her mate's gaze. She licked her lips and he moaned.

Then she pushed him back on the bed and positioned herself just right, taking him in her mouth and swirling her tongue around his head.

Jericho cursed and planted one hand beside her head, the other finding its way down her body, fingers teasing the entrance to her sex and finding her hot and ready. Erin moaned around his cock, letting her tongue explore all that she could.

But Jericho was big enough for it to be a challenge. Good thing she'd always be up for a bit of hard work.

She reveled in the way his body trembled, in every sound that escaped his mouth and the way his hand curled into the sheets right beside her, gripping so hard she wondered if they'd tear.

With a growl, Jericho pulled back, leaving Erin splayed out beneath him. His body was an inferno and a promise of eternal pleasure that she'd never give up.

He hiked her leg up over his shoulder and trailed kisses right down to the core of her, where he feasted like a starving man. Erin didn't try and stop the sensual sound that escaped her as she writhed under him. No matter how many times he tasted her, it would never be enough.

His gaze flicked up to meet her, blue eyes blazing with electric heat.

His tongue wove its own sensual spell around her until she could do nothing but beg for more and more and more as he brought her up and over the peak of pleasure, leaving her wrung out.

And yet.

Yes.

She still needed him. Still needed more.

She hauled him up, covering his mouth with her own and tasting her pleasure on his tongue. Jericho held onto her, his fingers clutching tight enough to really make her feel it.

Her leg hitched over his thigh, the hard length of him right there, so present and ready that Erin whimpered into the kiss.

She guided him to her entrance, the blunt head of his cock teasing her sensitive skin as he pushed in, finally joining them just as they were meant to be joined.

One thrust led to another, the sensation intoxicating and leaving Erin breathless. But still, she wanted more, needed harder. She clutched him tight, her nails digging in hard enough that his shirt would be covering the evidence of their lovemaking come morning.

The coil of pleasure tightened within her and snapped until Erin was soaring, her body surrendering completely to the pleasure of her mate.

Jericho cried out his own release, their bodies shuddering together as they lay entwined, heat and sweat and pleasure their only companions.

"You think you can handle another fifty years of this?" Erin teased, running her finger over her mate's chest.

He trapped her hand there and then raised her fingers to kiss them. "Fifty years? We'll just be getting started."

———

**Thank you for reading Wolf's Temptation!**
I'd appreciate it so much if you would consider leaving a review.

NEED A BIT MORE OF WOLF'S TEMPTATION?

Sign up at the link below to **receive TWO free bonus scenes** that didn't make it into the book.

**Scan the code to get your bonus scenes:**

**Congrats! You just finished the *Guarded by the***

**Shifter series! Looking for more paranormal romance?**

## CHECK OUT *THE ALPHA HEIST*

The alpha keeps what's his...

No one steals from Luke Torres. His fortress is legend and his pack of lions are deadly, ready to face any threat. When Luke meets Mel, she knocks his socks off with a scorching kiss, but when they meet again, they are captor and captive in a deadly game of cat vs. cat.

The thief is up to the task...

From the moment Mel takes the assignment, she knows that it should be impossible. But for the supernatural world's foremost thief, impossible is an irresistible challenge. Especially when the payment for this job will get her one step closer to revenge. When the job goes belly up, she finds herself in the lion's den and facing off with the most alluring man she's ever met.

Can she find a way to complete the job without losing her heart?

**Scan the code to learn more:**

# ALSO BY KATE RUDOLPH

**Guarded by the Shifter**

**Werewolf. Bodyguard. Mate.**
The origins of these shifters are shrouded in mystery, but they're determined to protect their mates from any harm that comes their way.
***Also available in audio!***
*Hunting Season*
*On the Prowl*
*Stalking Magic*
*Wolf Cursed*
*Hungry for the Wolf*
*Wolf's Temptation*

———

### Stealing the Alpha

**The thief takes what she wants, but the alpha keeps what's his...**

Join shifter thief Mel as she clashes with lion alpha Luke in an explosive trilogy of two opposites who can't keep away from one another.

***Also available in audio!***

*The Alpha Heist*
*Entangled with the Thief*
*In the Alpha's Bed*

————

### Alien Mates: Planet Exile

Guerran is no place for pretty human women. But these alien heroes will protect their mates!

**Also available in audio!**

Exile's Hunter
Exile's Adored

————

### Zulir Warrior Mates

**Kidnapped humans. Alien Warriors. Electric wings.**

The Zulir Warrior Mates series brings you human heroines and heroes abducted from Earth who find love – and wings! – with the alien warriors who rescue them.

***Also available in audio!***

*Synnr's Saint*

*Synnr's Hope*

*Synnr's Spark*

*Synnr's Kiss*

*Synnr's Ride*

––––––––

**Dragon Brides**

**Dragon Princes. Fierce Women. Love.**

Fated mates, fierce women, and dragon princes are ready to find their mates.

*Crux*

*Ranger*

*Saber*

*Cipher*

*Storm*

*Drake*

*Asher*

*Knox*

*Flint*

———

**Mated to the Alien**

**Fated Mate Alien Romance**

Detyens are doomed to die young if they don't find their fated mates.

Follow along as these mated pairs fight off aliens, corrupt dictators, prejudiced humans, pirates, and more! The books can be read or listened to in any order, though some characters show up in multiple stories.

***Select books available in audio.***

Pick a book and jump into the action today!

*Ruwen*

*Tyral*

*Stoan*

*Cyborg*

*Krayter*

*Kayleb*

*Shayn*

*Braxtyn*

*Doryan*

*Dekon*

———

## Detyen Warriors

**Detya was destroyed a hundred years ago. These doomed warriors are out to find justice… and their mates.**

The Detyen Warriors series brings you kick butt heroines, alpha alien heroes, fated mates, and relationships strong enough to span the galaxy!

**The entire series is also available in audio!**

*Soulless*

*Ruthless*

*Heartless*

*Faultless*

*Endless*

———

## Alien Holiday Romance

Christmas... in space????
These alien holiday romances look beyond Earth's winter holidays and ring in the season across the galaxy!
**Select titles available in audio.**
*Snowed in with the Alien Beast*
*The Alien's Winter Gift*
*The Alien Reindeer's Wild Ride*
*Trapped with her Alien Mate*

---

## Alien Outlaws

**Outlaws, schemes, and love... it's all there in the Alien Outlaws series...**

Andie Munster is sick of life on Ixilta, the planet she got dumped on after being abducted from Earth six years ago. And when the mysterious and dangerous Xandr shows up looking for a way off the planet, she's half-prisoner, half-co-conspirator in a wild rush to escape.

*Rogue Alien's Escape*
*Rogue Alien's Woman*
*Rogue Alien's Secret*
*Rogue Alien's Legacy*

---

***Find more by Kate Rudolph at*** www.
katerudolph.net

# ABOUT KATE RUDOLPH

KATE RUDOLPH IS paranormal and sci-fi romance writer who lives in Indiana. She loves writing about kick butt heroines and the steamy heroes who love them. She's been devouring romance novels since she was too young to be reading them and had to hide her books so no one would take them away. She couldn't imagine a better job in this world than writing romances and sharing them with her fellow readers.

If you enjoyed this story, please consider leaving a review.